the milk cotton baby collection

14 garment designs for ages 0-4 years using Rowan DK & Fine Milk Cotton
by Marie Wallin & Martin Storey with 7 accessories by Lisa Richardson

daisy romper

jack romper

polly cardi

kalli slippers & lucy shoes

faye cardi

eric cardi

beatrice dress, walter the elephant & la la teddy

alphabet blanket, alphabet blocks, la la teddy & waldo the wonder cat

freddy coat

tabitha cardi

lucy shoes

edith shrug

marcus slipover

jake hoodie

margo jumper

abel jumper

bob jumper

the milk cotton baby collection

GALLERY

walter the elephant 46

alphabet blanket 45

polly cardi 74

marcus slipover 72

lucy shoes 70

edith shrug 54

waldo the wonder cat 67

eric cardi 52

alphabet blocks 44

abel jumper by Marie Wallin

YARN

To fit age

	0-3	3-6	6-9	9-12	12-18 months	2	3	4 years
Rowan Milk Cotton DK								
A Aniseed 090	1	1	1	1	1	1	2	2 x 50gm
B Tutti Fruitti 087	1	1	1	1	1	2	2	2 x 50gm
C Fruit Salad 089	1	1	1	1	1	1	2	2 x 50gm
D Sherbert 080	1	1	1	1	1	2	2	2 x 50gm
E Bonfire Toffee 091	1	1	1	1	1	1	2	2 x 50gm
F Scented Satin 088	1	1	1	1	1	2	2	2 x 50gm

NEEDLES

1 pair 3¼mm (no 10) (US 3) needles & 1 pair 3¾mm (no 9) (US 5) needles

BUTTONS – 3 x 00405

TENSION

22 sts and 40 rows to 10 cm measured over g st using 3¾mm (US 5) needles.

STRIPE SEQUENCE

Rows 1 and 2: Using yarn A.
Rows 3 and 4: Using yarn B.
Rows 5 and 6: Using yarn C.
Rows 7 and 8: Using yarn D.
Rows 9 and 10: Using yarn E.
Rows 11 and 12: Using yarn F.
Rows 13 and 14: Using yarn B.
Rows 15 and 16: Using yarn D.
Rows 17 and 18: Using yarn C.
Rows 19 and 20: Using yarn A.
Rows 21 and 22: Using yarn E.
Rows 23 and 24: Using yarn B.
Rows 25 and 26: Using yarn F.
Rows 27 and 28: Using yarn D.
These 28 rows form stripe sequence and are repeated.

BACK

Using 3¾mm (US 5) needles and yarn A cast on 55 [57: 59: 61: 63: 67: 69: 71] sts.
Beg with row 1, work in g st in stripe sequence until back meas approx 15 [17: 17: 19: 19: 21: 21: 23] cm, ending after stripe row 4 [12: 12: 20: 20: 28: 28: 8] and with RS facing for next row.

Shape armholes

Keeping stripes correct, cast off 2 [2: 2: 2: 3: 3: 3: 3] sts at beg of next 2 rows. 51 [53: 55: 57: 57: 61: 63: 65] sts.
Dec 1 st at each end of next 1 [1: 1: 1: 1: 3: 3: 3] rows, then on foll 1 [1: 2: 2: 2: 1: 2: 2] alt rows. 47 [49: 49: 51: 51: 53: 53: 55] sts.**
Cont straight until armhole meas approx 10 [10: 11: 11: 12: 12: 13: 13] cm, ending after stripe row 16 [24: 28: 8: 12: 20: 24: 4] and with RS facing for next row.

Shape shoulders and back neck

Next row (RS): Cast off 5 [5: 5: 5: 5: 5: 5: 6] sts, K until there are 8 [8: 8: 9: 9: 9: 9: 9] sts on right needle and turn, leaving rem sts on a holder.
Work each side of neck separately.
Cast off 3 sts at beg of next row.
Cast off rem 5 [5: 5: 6: 6: 6: 6: 6] sts.
With RS facing, rejoin appropriate yarn to rem sts, cast off centre 21 [23: 23: 23: 23: 25: 25: 25] sts, K to end.
Complete to match first side, reversing shapings.

FRONT

Work as given for back to **.
Work 15 [13: 14: 14: 15: 15: 17: 13] rows, ending after stripe row 24 [2: 5: 13: 14: 22: 26: 2] and with RS [RS: WS: WS: RS: RS: RS: RS] facing for next row.

Shape opening

Place marker at left armhole edge of last row to denote base of opening.
Keeping stripes correct, dec 1 st at marked edge of next 8 [8: 9: 9: 10: 10: 10: 12] rows, ending after stripe row 4 [10: 14: 22: 24: 4: 8: 14] and with RS facing for next row. 39 [41: 40: 42: 41: 43: 43: 43] sts.

Shape neck

Next row (RS): K2tog, K7 and turn, leaving rem sts on a holder.
Work each side of neck separately.
Keeping stripes correct, dec 1 st at each end of next 3 rows, ending after stripe row 8 [14: 18: 26: 28: 8: 12: 18] and with RS facing for next row. 2 sts.
Next row (RS): K2tog and fasten off.
With RS facing, rejoin appropriate yarn to rem sts, cast off centre 13 [15: 13: 15: 13: 15: 15: 13] sts, K to end.

Keeping stripes correct, dec 1 st at neck edge of next 6 rows, then on foll 1 [1: 2: 1: 2: 2: 2: 3] alt rows. 10 [10: 10: 11: 11: 11: 11: 12] sts.
Work 4 [6: 4: 6: 6: 6: 6: 6] rows, ending after stripe row 17 [25: 1: 9: 13: 21: 25: 5] and with WS facing for next row

Shape shoulder

Cast off 5 [5: 5: 5: 5: 5: 5: 6] sts at beg of next and foll alt row.
Work 1 row.
Cast off rem 5 [5: 5: 6: 6: 6: 6: 6] sts.

LEFT SHOULDER PANEL

Using 3¾mm (US 5) needles and yarn F [B: C: B: D: B: D: B] cast on 2 sts.
Beg with row 25 [3: 6: 14: 15: 23: 27: 3] and RS [RS: WS: WS: RS: RS: RS: RS] facing, work in g st in stripe sequence as folls:
Inc 1 st at end [end: beg: beg: end: end: end: end] of next row.
Place marker at beg [beg: end: end: beg: beg: beg: beg] of last row.
Inc 1 st at unmarked edge of next 11 [11: 12: 12: 13: 13: 13: 15] rows, ending after stripe row 8 [14: 18: 26: 28: 8: 12: 18] and with RS facing for next row. 14 [14: 15: 15: 16: 16: 16: 18] sts.
Place another marker at shaped (neck) edge of last row.

Shape neck

Keeping stripes correct, dec 1 st at neck edge of next 3 rows, then on foll 1 [1: 2: 1: 2: 2: 2: 3] alt rows. 10 [10: 10: 11: 11: 11: 11: 12] sts.
Work 3 [5: 3: 5: 5: 5: 5: 5] rows, ending after stripe row 16 [24: 28: 8: 12: 20: 24: 4] and with RS facing for next row

Shape shoulder

Cast off 5 [5: 5: 5: 5: 5: 5: 6] sts at beg of next and foll alt row.
Work 1 row.
Cast off rem 5 [5: 5: 6: 6: 6: 6: 6] sts.

SLEEVES

Using 3¾mm (US 5) needles and yarn B [E: A: A: E: C: E: C] cast on 27 [29: 29: 31: 31: 33: 33: 35] sts.
Beg with row 13 [9: 1: 1: 21: 17: 9: 5], work in g st in stripe sequence (see above), shaping sides by inc 1 st at each end of 3rd [5th: 5th: 5th: 5th: 7th: 5th: 7th] and every foll 4th [6th: 6th: 6th: 6th: 8th: 6th: 8th] row to 39 [37: 45: 35: 51: 53: 45: 49] sts, then on every foll 6th [8th: 8th: 8th: 8th: -: 8th: 10th] row until there are 43 [43: 47: 47: 53: -: 57: 57] sts.
Cont straight until sleeve meas approx 12 [15: 17: 19: 21: 24: 26: 29] cm, ending after stripe row 4 [12: 12: 20: 20: 28: 28: 8] and with RS facing for next row.

Shape top

Keeping stripes correct, cast off 3 [3: 2: 2: 2: 2: 2: 2] sts at beg of next 4 [4: 4: 4: 6: 6: 16: 16] rows, then 4 [4: 3: 3: 3: 3: 3: 3] sts at beg of foll 4 [4: 8: 8: 8: 8: 2: 2] rows.
Cast off rem 15 [15: 15: 15: 17: 17: 19: 19] sts.

MAKING UP

Press as described on the information page.
Join right shoulder seam using back stitch, or mattress stitch if preferred.

Left button border

With RS facing, using 3¼mm (US 3) needles and yarn F, pick up and knit 14 [14: 15: 15: 16: 16: 16: 18] sts evenly along lower shaped edge of left shoulder panel, from marker at neck edge to cast-on edge.
Work in g st for 3 rows, inc 1 st at armhole edge of every row and ending with WS facing for next row. 17 [17: 18: 18: 19: 19: 19: 21] sts.
Cast off knitwise (on WS).

Left buttonhole border

With RS facing, using 3¼mm (US 3) needles and yarn F, pick up and knit 14 [14: 15: 15: 16: 16: 16: 18] sts evenly along shaped left front shoulder edge, from marker at armhole to fasten-off point at neck edge.
Row 1 (WS): K to last 2 sts, K2tog.
Row 2: K2tog, K3 [3: 4: 4: 3: 3: 3: 5], yfwd, K2tog, K3 [3: 3: 3: 4: 4: 4: 4], yfwd, K2tog, K1 [1: 1: 1: 2: 2: 2: 2].
Row 3: As row 1.
Row 4: K2tog, K to end. 10 [10: 11: 11: 12: 12: 12: 14] sts.
Cast off knitwise (on WS).
Lay buttonhole border over button border so that markers along armhole edges match and sew together along armhole edge.
Join left shoulder seam.

Neckband

With RS facing, using 3¼mm (US 3) needles and yarn F, beg and ending at top of borders, pick up and knit 9 sts down left side of neck, 13 [15: 13: 15: 13: 15: 15: 13] sts from front, 12 [14: 14: 14: 16: 16: 16: 18] sts up right side of neck, 27 [29: 29: 29: 29: 31: 31: 31] sts from back, then 11 [13: 13: 15: 15: 15: 15: 17] sts down neck edge of left shoulder panel. 72 [80: 78: 82: 82: 86: 86: 88] sts.
Row 1 (WS): Knit.
Row 2: K2, K2tog, yfwd, K to end.
Work in g st for a further 3 rows, ending with RS facing for next row.
Beg with a K row, work in st st for 4 rows, ending with RS facing for next row
Cast off.
See information page for finishing instructions, setting in sleeves using the shallow set-in method.

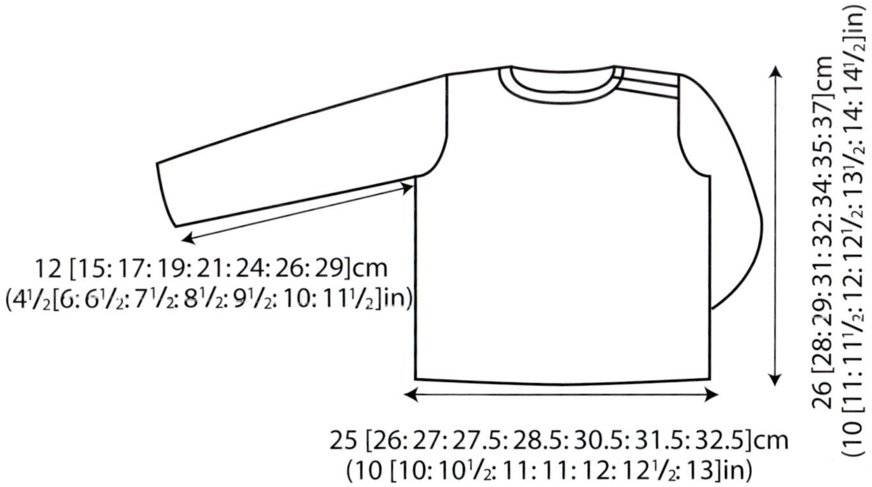

beatrice dress by Marie Wallin

YARN

To fit age

	0-3	3-6	6-9	9-12	12-18	months	2	3	4 years
Rowan Fine Milk Cotton									
	3	3	4	4	4		5	5	5 x 50gm

Small amount of Milk Cotton in 4 contrast colours for embroidery (photographed in Barley Sugar 481 with embroidery in Milk Cotton DK, Snow 093, Bubble Gum 086, Fruit Salad 089 and Aniseed 090)

NEEDLES

1 pair 2¾mm (no 12) (US 2) needles
2.00mm (no 14) (US B1) crochet hook

BUTTONS – 3 x 00320

TENSION

30 sts and 38 rows to 10 cm measured over st st using 2¾mm (US 2) needles.

UK CROCHET ABBREVIATIONS

ch = chain; ss = slip stitch; dc = double crochet; tr = treble.

BACK

Using 2¾mm (US 2) needles cast on 100 [106: 110: 118: 122: 130: 132: 138] sts.
Beg with a K row, work in st st, shaping sides by dec 1 st at each end of 11th [11th: 9th: 9th: 7th: 7th: 11th: 11th] and every foll 6th row until 74 [78: 80: 84: 86: 90: 92: 96] sts rem.
Work 7 rows, ending with RS facing for next row.
Next row (eyelet row) (RS): K4 [6: 2: 4: 5: 2: 3: 5], yfwd, K2tog, *K3, yfwd, K2tog, rep from * to last 3 [5: 1: 3: 4: 1: 2: 4] sts, K3 [5: 1: 3: 4: 1: 2: 4].
Cont straight until back meas 27 [29: 30: 33: 34: 37: 38: 40] cm, ending with RS facing for next row.
Shape armholes
Cast off 3 sts at beg of next 2 rows.
68 [72: 74: 78: 80: 84: 86: 90] sts.**
Divide for back opening
Next row (RS): K2tog, K30 [32: 33: 35: 36: 38: 39: 41] and turn, leaving rem sts on a holder.
Work each side of neck separately.
Next row (WS): Cast on and K 4 sts, P to last 2 sts, P2tog.
34 [36: 37: 39: 40: 42: 43: 45] sts.
Next row: K2tog, K to end.
Next row: K4, P to last 0 [0: 0: 0: 0: 2: 2: 2] sts, (P2tog) 0 [0: 0: 0: 0: 1: 1: 1] times. 33 [35: 36: 38: 39: 40: 41: 43] sts.
Last 2 rows set the sts - back opening edge 4 sts in g st with all other sts in st st.
Keeping sts correct as set, dec 1 st at armhole edge of next and foll 0 [2: 2: 3: 3: 4: 4: 5] alt rows.
32 [32: 33: 34: 35: 35: 36: 37] sts.
Cont straight until armhole meas 10 [10: 11: 11: 12: 12: 13: 13] cm, ending with WS facing for next row.
Shape back neck and shoulder
Cast off 18 [19: 19: 19: 19: 20: 20: 21] sts at beg of next row, 5 [5: 5: 6: 6: 6: 6: 6] sts at beg of foll row, then 3 sts at beg of next row.
Cast off rem 6 [5: 6: 6: 7: 6: 7: 7] sts.
Mark positions of 3 buttons along right back opening edge - top button 1 cm below neck shaping, and rem 2 buttons evenly spaced between top button and base of back opening.
With RS facing, rejoin yarn to rem sts, K to last 2 sts, K2tog.
Next row (WS): P2tog, P to last 4 sts, K4.
Next row: K to last 2 sts, K2tog. 33 [35: 36: 38: 39: 41: 42: 44] sts.
These 2 rows set the sts - back opening edge 4 sts in g st with all other sts in st st.
Complete to match first side, reversing shapings and making 3 buttonholes to correspond with positions marked for buttons as folls:
Buttonhole row (RS): K1, K2tog, yfwd (to make a buttonhole), K to end (working armhole dec if appropriate).

FRONT

Work as given for back to **.
Dec 1 st at each end of next 3 [3: 3: 3: 3: 5: 5: 5] rows, then on foll 1 [3: 3: 4: 4: 4: 4: 5] alt rows. 60 [60: 62: 64: 66: 66: 68: 70] sts.
Cont straight until 14 [16: 16: 16: 18: 18: 18: 20] rows less have been worked than on back to beg of shoulder shaping, ending with RS facing for next row.
Shape neck
Next row (RS): K19 [19: 20: 21: 23: 22: 23: 24] and turn, leaving rem sts on a holder.
Work each side of neck separately.
Dec 1 st at neck edge of next 6 rows, then on foll 2 [3: 3: 3: 4: 4: 4: 5] alt rows. 11 [10: 11: 12: 13: 12: 13: 13] sts.
Work 3 rows, ending with RS facing for next row.

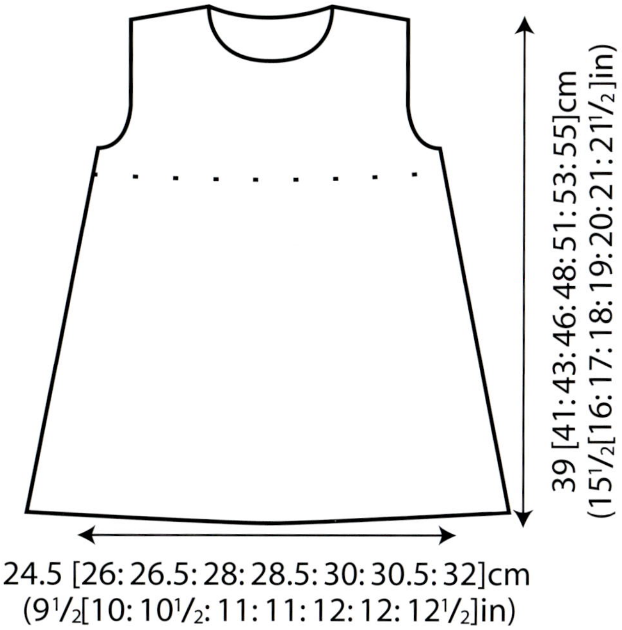

Shape shoulder
Cast off 5 [5: 5: 6: 6: 6: 6: 6] sts at beg of next row.
Work 1 row.
Cast off rem 6 [5: 6: 6: 7: 6: 7: 7] sts.
With RS facing, rejoin yarn to rem sts, cast off centre 22 [22: 22: 22: 20: 22: 22: 22] sts, K to end.
Complete to match first side, reversing shapings.

MAKING UP

Press as described on the information page.
Join both shoulder seams using back stitch, or mattress stitch if preferred. Sew cast-on edge at base of right back opening edge in place behind left back opening edge. Join side seams.

Hem edging
With WS facing and using 2.00mm (US B1) crochet hook, attach yarn at base of one side seam, 1 ch (does NOT count as st), work 1 round of dc evenly all round cast-on edge, ensuring an even number of dc is worked and ending with ss to first dc, turn.
Next round (RS): 1 ss into first dc, *2 ch, 3 tr into next dc, 2 ch, 1 ss into next dc, rep from * to end, working ss at end of last rep into same place as ss at beg of round.
Fasten off.

Armhole edgings (both alike)
Work as given for hem edging, attaching yarn at top of side seam.

Neck edging
With WS facing and using 2.00mm (US B1) crochet hook, attach yarn at top of right back opening edge, 1 ch (does NOT count as st), work 1 row of dc evenly all round entire neck edge, ensuring an odd number of dc is worked, turn.
Next row (RS): 1 ss into first dc, *2 ch, 3 tr into next dc, 2 ch, 1 ss into next dc, rep from * to end.
Fasten off.

Tie
Using 2.00mm (US B1) crochet hook make 3 ch.
Row 1: 1 dc into 2nd ch from hook, 1 dc into next ch, turn. 2 sts.
Row 2: 1 ch (does NOT count as st), 1 dc into each of next 2 sts, turn.
Rep last row until tie meas 81 [84: 87: 91: 94: 97: 100: 104] cm.
Fasten off.
Using photograph as a guide, thread tie through eyelet row and tie ends in a bow at centre front.

Embroidery
Using photograph as a guide, embroider floral design around hem and front neck edges. For flowers, work 5 lazy daisy stitches radiating out from one point using cream, and french knot flower centre using pink. Embroider bullion knots between and next to each flower using orange, then 2 overlaid cross stitches in green between this second row of bullion knots. The contrast embroidery DK yarn is split in order to acheive a fine finish.
See information page for finishing instructions.

alphabet blanket by Lisa Richardson

YARN
Rowan Milk Cotton DK
14 x 50gm
(photographed in either Barley Sugar 081 or Sherbert 080)

NEEDLES
1 pair 3¼mm (no 10) (US 3) needles
1 pair 3¾mm (no 9) (US 5) needles

TENSION
22 sts and 30 rows to 10 cm measured over st st, 24 sts and 39 rows to 10 cm measured over moss st, both using 3¾mm (US 5) needles.

FINISHED SIZE
Completed blanket meas 77 cm x 117 cm (30½ ins x 46 ins).

MOSS ST SQUARES (make 27)
Using 3¾mm (US 5) needles cast on 30 sts.
Row 1 (RS): K2, *P2, K2, rep from * to end.
Rows 2 and 3: P2, *K2, P2, rep from * to end.
Row 4: As row 1.
These 4 rows form moss st.
Cont in moss st until square meas 12 cm, ending with RS facing for next row.
Cast off in moss st.

FANCY SQUARES (make 27)
Using 3¾mm (US 5) needles cast on 27 sts.
Now work 36 rows foll chart, ending with RS facing for next row.
Work a further 26 squares using the blank chart from Alphabet blocks pattern to make the remaining letters, making 27 different squares.

MAKING UP
Press as described on the information page.
Alternating moss st and fancy squares to create a checkerboard effect, join all 54 squares together to form one large rectangle 6 squares wide and 9 squares long.
Side borders (both alike)
With RS facing and using 3¼mm (US 3) needles, pick up and knit 250 sts evenly along one long edge of joined squares.
Beg with row 1, work in moss st as given for moss st squares, inc 1 st at each end of 2nd and foll 3 alt rows, taking inc sts into patt and ending with WS facing for next row. 258 sts.
Work 1 row.
Dec 1 st at each end of next and foll 3 alt rows. 250 sts.
Work 1 row, ending with RS facing for next row.
Cast off.
End borders (both alike)
With RS facing and using 3¼mm (US 3) needles, pick up and knit 166 sts evenly along one short edge of joined blocks.
Beg with row 1, work in moss st as given for moss st squares, inc 1 st at each end of 2nd and foll 3 alt rows, taking inc sts into patt and ending with WS facing for next row. 174 sts.
Work 1 row.
Dec 1 st at each end of next and foll 3 alt rows. 166 sts.
Work 1 row, ending with RS facing for next row.
Cast off.
Join shaped row-end edges of borders, then fold border in half.
Slip stitch neatly in place to pick-up rows.

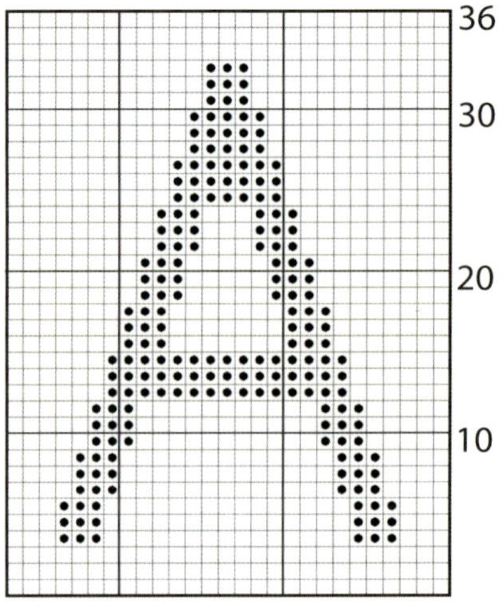

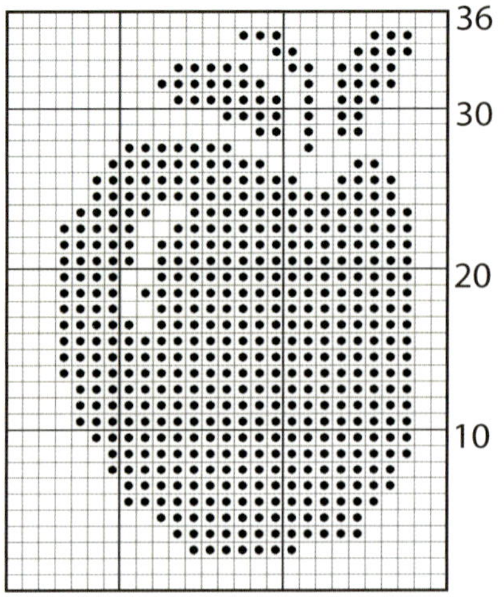

Blanket Key
☐ K on RS, P on WS
● P on RS, K on WS

alphabet blocks by Lisa Richardson

YARN
Rowan Milk Cotton DK
A 1 x 50gm
B 1 x 50gm
(photographed in Aniseed 090 (A) and Fruit Salad 089 (B), Dip Dab 085 (A) and Shrimps 083 (B), Tutti Fruitti 087 (A) and Scented Satin 088 (B), Bubble Gum 086 (A) and Barley Sugar 081 (B), and Bonfire Toffee 091 (A) and Snow 093 (B))

NEEDLES
1 pair 3¾mm (no 9) (US 5) needles

EXTRAS — one 12 cm foam cube for each block (or washable toy filling)

TENSION
22 sts and 30 rows to 10 cm measured over st st, 24 sts and 39 rows to 10 cm measured over moss st, both using 3¾mm (US 5) needles.

FINISHED SIZE
Each completed block meas 12 cm (4¾ ins) along all edges.

MOSS ST SQUARES

Using 3¾mm (US 5) needles and yarn A cast on 30 sts.
Row 1 (RS): K2, *P2, K2, rep from * to end.
Rows 2 and 3: P2, *K2, P2, rep from * to end.
Row 4: As row 1.
These 4 rows form moss st.
Cont in moss st until square meas 12 cm, ending with RS facing for next row.
Cast off in moss st.
Make a second square using yarn B.

FANCY SQUARES

Using 3¾mm (US 5) needles and yarn A cast on 27 sts.
Now work 36 rows foll desired chart (using blank chart to make further letters), ending with RS facing for next row — for these reps of charts, entire chart is worked in st st, beg with a K row, using yarn A for background and yarn B for design.
Make a second square in this way, reversing position of colours and choosing a different chart.

STRIPED SQUARES

Using 3¾mm (US 5) needles and yarn A cast on 27 sts.
Beg with a K row, work in striped st st as folls:
Rows 1 and 2: Using yarn A.
Rows 3 and 4: Using yarn B.
These 4 rows form striped st st.
Cont in striped st st until square meas 12 cm, ending with RS facing for next row.
Cast off in moss st.
Make a second square in exactly the same way.

MAKING UP

Press as described on the information page.
Sew 5 of the squares together to form an open box shape. Insert foam (or toy filling), then attach rem 6th square to form completed block.

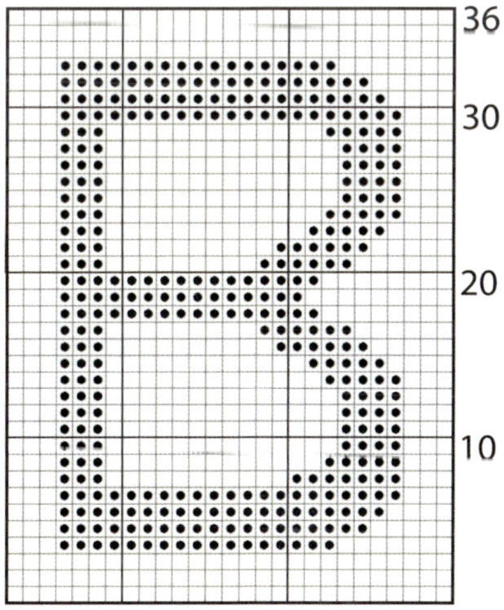

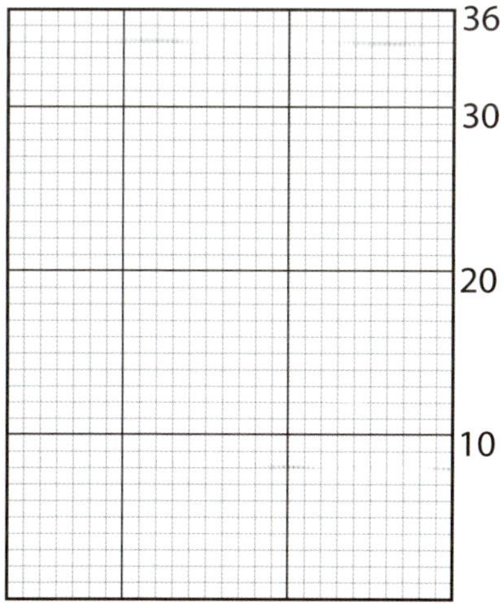

walter the elephant by Lisa Richardson

YARN
Rowan Milk Cotton DK
3 x 50gm
(photographed in Snow 093)

NEEDLES
1 pair 3¼mm (no 10) (US 3) needles

EXTRAS - Washable toy filling. 20 cm x 30 cm piece of printed cotton fabric

TENSION
26 sts and 34 rows to 10 cm measured over st st using 3¼mm (US 3) needles.

FINISHED SIZE
Completed toy is approx 36 cm (14 ins) from head to tail.

FIRST SIDE

Trunk
Using 3¼mm (US 3) needles cast on 4 sts.
Beg with a P row, work in rev st st throughout as folls:
Work 1 row, ending with WS facing for next row.
Inc 1 st at each end of next 2 rows, then 1 st at end of foll row. 9 sts.
Work 2 rows, ending with RS facing for next row.
Dec 1 st at beg of next and foll alt row, then at same edge on foll 3 rows and at same time inc 1 st at end of next and foll 4th row. 6 sts.
Work 14 rows, ending with RS facing for next row.
Inc 1 st at beg of next and foll alt row, then at same edge on foll 5 rows, ending with RS facing for next row. 13 sts.
Break yarn and leave sts on a holder.

****Back leg**
Using 3¼mm (US 3) needles cast on 16 sts.
Beg with a K row, work in st st throughout as folls:
Work 2 rows, ending with RS facing for next row.
Dec 1 st at end of next and foll alt row and at same time dec 1 st at beg of 3rd row. 13 sts.
Work 5 rows, ending with RS facing for next row.
Inc 1 st at end of next and 3 foll alt rows, then at same edge of foll 12 rows, ending with WS facing for next row, and at same time dec 1 st at beg of next and 3 foll 6th rows. 25 sts.
Cast on 4 sts at beg of next and foll alt row. 33 sts.
Work 1 row, ending with WS facing for next row.
Break yarn and leave sts on a holder.

Front leg
Using 3¼mm (US 3) needles cast on 16 sts.
Beg with a K row, work in st st throughout as folls:
Work 1 row, ending with WS facing for next row.
Dec 1 st at end of next 2 rows. 14 sts.
Work 1 row, ending with RS facing for next row.
Inc 1 st at beg of next and 9 foll alt rows, then at same edge of foll 7 rows, ending with RS facing for next row, and at same time dec 1 st at end of next and foll 12 alt rows. 18 sts.
Cast on 4 sts at beg and dec 1 st at end of next row. 21 sts.
Work 1 row.
Cast on 4 sts at beg and dec 1 st at end of next row, ending with WS facing for next row. 24 sts.

Join legs
Next row (WS): K 24 sts of front leg, turn and cast on 15 sts, turn and K 33 sts of back leg. 72 sts.
Dec 1 st at beg of next and foll 6th row. 70 sts.
Work 1 row, ending with RS facing for next row.**
Row 43 (RS): K56, P14.
Row 44: K14, P56.
Row 45: K42, P27, inc in last st. 71 sts.
Row 46: K29, P42.
Row 47: K28, P42, inc in last st. 72 sts.
Row 48: K44, P28.
Row 49: K14, P57, inc in last st. 73 sts.
Row 50: K59, P14.

Join trunk
Row 51 (RS): P all 73 sts of body section, turn and cast on 4 sts, turn and P across 13 sts of trunk section. 90 sts.
Beg with a K row, now work all sts in rev st as folls:
Work 1 row, ending with RS facing for next row.
Inc 1 st at end of next and 4 foll 4th rows and at same time dec 1 st at beg of 11th and foll 3 alt rows. 91 sts.
Work 1 row, ending with RS facing for next row.
Dec 1 st at beg of next row and at same edge on foll 3 rows, ending with RS facing for next row, and at same time dec 1 st at end of 3rd row. 86 sts.

Shape top of back
Next row (RS): P2tog, P36 and turn, leaving rem 48 sts on a holder.
Work on this set of 37 sts only for top of back.
Dec 1 st at end of next row and at same edge on foll 2 rows and at same time cast off 6 sts at beg of next and foll alt row. 22 sts.
Cast off 6 sts at beg of next 2 rows, ending with RS facing for next row.

Cast off rem 10 sts.
Shape top of head
Rejoin yarn to 48 sts on holder with RS facing, cast off next 15 sts, P to end. 33 sts.
Dec 1 st at end of next row, ending with RS facing for next row. 32 sts.
Dec 1 st at beg of next and foll 4 alt rows, then at same edge on foll 3 rows and at same time dec 1 st at end of next and foll 4th row, then on foll 2 alt rows, then at same edge on foll 3 rows, ending with RS facing for next row. 17 sts.
Cast off 4 sts at beg and dec 1 st at end of next row. 12 sts.
Cast off 5 sts at beg of next row.
Cast off rem 7 sts.

SECOND SIDE
Work exactly as given for first side – sides are identical so position of rev st st and st st sections is reversed on one side to that on the other side.

GUSSET
Work as given for first side from ** to **.
Row 43 (RS): K56, wrap next st (by slipping next st on left needle onto right needle, taking yarn to opposite side of work between needles and then slipping same st back onto left needle – when working back across wrapped sts work the wrapped st and the wrapping loop together) and turn.
Row 44 and every foll alt row: P to end.
Row 45: K42, wrap next st and turn.
Row 47: K28, wrap next st and turn.
Row 49: K14, wrap next st and turn.
Row 51: K to end.
Place markers at both ends of last row.
Row 53: As row 49.
Row 55: As row 47.
Row 57: As row 45.
Row 59: As row 43.
Row 60: P to end.
Work 2 rows, ending with RS facing for next row.
Inc 1 st at beg of next and foll 6th row, ending with WS facing for next row. 72 sts.
Shape second inner front leg
Next row (WS): P24 and turn, leaving rem 48 sts on a holder.
Work on this set of 24 sts only for second inner front leg.
Cast off 4 sts at beg of next and foll alt row and at same time inc 1 st at end of next and foll alt row. 18 sts.
Dec 1 st at end of next row and at same edge of foll 7 rows, then on foll 9 alt rows and at same time inc 1 st at end of 2nd and foll 12 alt rows. 14 sts.
Work 1 row, ending with RS facing for next row.
Inc 1 st at end of next 2 rows, ending with RS facing for next row.
Cast off rem 16 sts.
Shape second inner back leg
Rejoin yarn to 48 sts left on holder with WS facing, cast off 15 sts, P to end. 33 sts.
Work 1 row, ending with WS facing for next row.
Cast off 4 sts at beg of next and foll alt row, ending with RS facing for next row. 25 sts.
Inc 1 st at beg of next and 3 foll 6th rows and at same time dec 1 st at end of next row and at same edge on foll 12 rows, then on foll 3 alt rows. 13 sts.
Work 5 rows, ending with RS facing for next row.
Inc 1 st at both ends of next row, then at end only of foll alt row.
Work 1 row, ending with RS facing for next row.
Cast off rem 16 sts.

EARS (make 2)
Using 3¼mm (US 3) needles cast on 6 sts.
Beg with a K row, work in st st throughout as folls:
Work 1 row, ending with WS facing for next row.
Row 2 (WS): Inc twice in first st, P to last st, inc once in last st. 9 sts.
Row 3: Inc once in first st, K to last st, inc twice in last st. 12 sts.
Row 4: As row 2. 15 sts.
Inc 1 st at end of next row and at same edge on foll 2 rows. 18 sts.
Work 6 rows, ending with WS facing for next row.
Dec 1 st at end of next row. 17 sts.
Work 2 rows, ending with RS facing for next row.
Inc 1 st at end of next row. 18 sts.
Work 1 row.
Dec 1 st at beg of next row. 17 sts.
Work 5 rows, ending with RS facing for next row.
Inc 1 st at beg of next row. 18 sts.
Work 2 rows, ending with WS facing for next row.
Cast off 2 sts at beg of next row. 16 sts.
Dec 1 st at end of next row and at same edge on foll 5 rows, ending with RS facing for next row, and at same time dec 1 st at beg of 3rd and foll alt row, then at same edge on foll row.
Cast off rem 7 sts.
Make a second ear in the same way but reading K for P and vice versa (to reverse RS of work and thereby make a pair).

MAKING UP
Press as described on the information page.
From fabric, cut out a pair of ear shapes same size as knitted ears, adding seam allowance along all edges. Cut out four 3.5 cm x 4 cm oval pieces, adding seam allowance around entire outer edge, for base of feet. For eyes, cut out two 2 cm x 2.5 cm oval shapes, adding seam allowance around entire outer edge. For tusks, cut out two triangles measuring 5.5 cm along 2 edges and 3 cm along 3rd edge, adding seam allowance around entire outer edge.
Leaving cast-on edges open, sew first part of gusset to one side piece, matching shaped edges and stopping at ends of marked gusset row – join pieces along front, back and inside leg and belly edges. In same way, join rem edges of gusset to other side piece, leaving gusset cast-off and side cast-on edges open. Join sides together along entire front neck, trunk, head, back and bottom edges, leaving an opening to insert toy filling. Insert toy filling so elephant is firmly filled and sew opening closed.
Fold seam allowance to WS around outer edge of each base of foot piece. Sew folded edges to open edges of knitting at base of legs, inserting a little more toy filling to ensure legs are firmly filled.
Sew fabric ears to knitted ears along entire outer edge, leaving an opening. Turn ears RS out and close opening. Attach to sides of head as in photograph.
Fold seam allowance to WS around outer edge of each eye piece. Attach to head as in photograph.
Fold each tusk piece in half and sew along longer edge to form a cone shape. Turn RS out and insert toy filling.
Fold in raw edges at opening edge, then sew tusks to head as in photograph.
Make a 5 cm long plait and knot one end, leaving a 4 cm tassel. Attach plait to back as in photograph to form tail.

daisy & jack romper

by Marie Wallin

YARN

To fit age

		0-3	3-6	6-9	9-12	12-18	months
Rowan Fine Milk Cotton							
	Daisy		Jack				
A	Shrimps 483		Humbugs 484				
		3	3	4	4	4	x 50gm
B	Snow 493		Snow 493				
		1	1	1	1	1	x 50gm

NEEDLES

1 pair 2mm (no 14) (US 0) needles
1 pair 2¾mm (no 12) (US 2) needles

BUTTONS – 8 x 00322

TENSION

30 sts and 38 rows to 10 cm measured over st st using 2¾mm (US 2) needles.
27 sts and 49 rows to 10 cm measured over moss st using 2¾mm (US 2) needles.

BACK

First leg

Using 2mm (US 0) needles and yarn B cast on 27 [29: 31: 33: 35] sts.

Row 1 (RS): K1, *P1, K1, rep from * to end.

Row 2: As row 1.

These 2 rows form moss st.

Work in moss st for a further 7 rows, ending with WS facing for next row.

Row 10 (WS): Moss st 4 [4: 4: 5: 5] sts, inc in next st, (moss st 7 [8: 9: 9: 10] sts, inc in next st) twice, moss st 4 [4: 4: 5: 5] sts, cast off rem 2 sts. 28 [30: 32: 34: 36] sts.

Break off yarn B and join in yarn A.

Change to 2¾mm (US 2) needles.

Beg with a K row, work in st st, shaping inside leg by inc 1 st at beg of 3rd and 0 [0: 0: 0: 2] foll 6th rows, then on 0 [1: 3: 4: 2] foll 4th rows, then on 8 [7: 4: 3: 2] foll alt rows, ending with WS facing for next row. 37 [39: 40: 42: 43] sts.

Inc 1 st at shaped inside leg edge of next 3 rows, ending with RS facing for next row. 40 [42: 43: 45: 46] sts.

Break yarn and leave sts on a holder.

Second leg

Using 2mm (US 0) needles and yarn B cast on 27 [29: 31: 33: 35] sts.

Work in moss st as given for first leg for 9 rows, ending with WS facing for next row.

****Row 10 (WS):** Cast off 2 sts, moss st until there are 4 [4: 4: 5: 5] sts on right needle after cast-off, inc in next st, (moss st 7 [8: 9: 9: 10] sts, inc in next st) twice, moss st 4 [4: 4: 5: 5] sts. 28 [30: 32: 34: 36] sts.

Break off yarn B and join in yarn A.

Change to 2¾mm (US 2) needles.

Beg with a K row, work in st st, shaping inside leg by inc 1 st at end of 3rd and 0 [0: 0: 0: 2] foll 6th rows, then on 0 [1: 3: 4: 2] foll 4th rows, then on 8 [7: 4: 3: 2] foll alt rows, ending with WS facing for next row. 37 [39: 40: 42: 43] sts.

Inc 1 st at shaped inside leg edge of next 3 rows, ending with RS facing for next row. 40 [42: 43: 45: 46] sts.

Join legs

Next row (RS): K 40 [42: 43: 45: 46] sts of second leg, turn and cast on 11 sts, turn and K 40 [42: 43: 45: 46] sts of first leg. 91 [95: 97: 101: 103] sts.

Work 9 [11: 13: 15: 17] rows, ending with RS facing for next row.

Dec 1 st at each end of next and every foll 8th row until 75 [79: 81: 85: 87] sts rem.

Cont straight until back meas 28 [29: 30: 31: 32] cm from leg cast-on edges, ending with WS facing for next row.

Next row (WS): P5 [3: 4: 3: 4], P2tog, (P7 [8: 8: 9: 9], P2tog) 7 times, P to end. 67 [71: 73: 77: 79] sts.**

Work in moss st for 14 rows, ending with RS facing for next row.

Shape raglans

Cast off 2 sts at beg of next 2 rows. 63 [67: 69: 73: 75] sts.

Dec 1 st at each end of next row. 61 [65: 67: 71: 73] sts.

Work 1 row, ending with RS facing for next row.

Divide for back opening

Next row (RS): (Work 2 tog) 0 [0: 1: 1: 1] times, moss st 28 [30: 29: 31: 32] sts and turn, leaving rem sts on a holder.

Work each side of neck separately.

Cast on 5 sts at beg of next row. 33 [35: 35: 37: 38] sts.

Dec 1 st at raglan armhole edge of next [next: 3rd: next: next] and foll 0 [0: 0: 2: 3] alt rows, then on every foll 4th row until 20 [21: 21: 21: 21] sts rem.

Work 3 rows, ending with RS facing for next row.

Cast off.

Mark positions of 3 buttons along right back opening edge - top button 1 cm below neck shaping, and rem 2 buttons evenly spaced between top button and base of back opening.
With RS facing, rejoin yarn to rem sts, moss st to last 0 [0: 2: 2: 2] sts, (work 2 tog) 0 [0: 1: 1: 1] times. 33 [35: 35: 37: 38] sts.
Complete to match first side, reversing shapings and making 3 buttonholes to correspond with positions marked for buttons as folls:
Buttonhole row (RS): Moss st 1 st, work 2 tog, yrn (to make a buttonhole), moss st to end (working raglan armhole dec if appropriate).

FRONT

First leg

Using 2mm (US 0) needles and yarn B cast on 27 [29: 31: 33: 35] sts.
Work in moss st as given for first leg of back for 4 rows, ending with RS facing for next row.
Row 5 (RS): Moss st 1 st, work 2 tog, yrn (to make a buttonhole), moss st to end.
Work in moss st for a further 4 rows, ending with WS facing for next row.
Row 10 (WS): Moss st 4 [4: 4: 5: 5] sts, inc in next st, (moss st 7 [8: 9: 9: 10] sts, inc in next st) twice, moss st 4 [4: 4: 5: 5] sts, cast off rem 2 sts. 28 [30: 32: 34: 36] sts.
Break off yarn B and join in yarn A.
Change to 2¾mm (US 2) needles.
Beg with a K row, work in st st, shaping inside leg by inc 1 st at beg of 3rd and 0 [0: 0: 0: 2] foll 6th rows, then on 0 [1: 3: 4: 2] foll 4th rows, then on 8 [7: 4: 3: 2] foll alt rows, ending with WS facing for next row. 37 [39: 40: 42: 43] sts.
Inc 1 st at shaped inside leg edge of next 3 rows, ending with RS facing for next row. 40 [42: 43: 45: 46] sts.
Break yarn and leave sts on a holder.

Second leg

Using 2mm (US 0) needles and yarn B cast on 27 [29: 31: 33: 35] sts.
Work in moss st as given for first leg for 4 rows, ending with RS facing for next row.
Row 5 (RS): Moss st to last 3 sts, yrn (to make a buttonhole), work 2 tog, moss st 1 st.
Work in moss st for a further 4 rows, ending with WS facing for next row.
Work as given for back from ** to **.
Work in moss st for 3 rows, ending with WS facing for next row.
Next row (WS): Moss st 33 [35: 36: 38: 39] sts, inc in next st, moss st to end. 68 [72: 74: 78: 80] sts.

Place chart

Next row (RS): Moss st 24 [26: 27: 29: 30] sts, work next 20 sts as row 1 of chart, moss st to end.
Next row: Moss st 24 [26: 27: 29: 30] sts, work next 20 sts as row 2 of chart, moss st to end.
These 2 rows set position of chart.
Cont as set for a further 8 rows, ending with RS facing for next row.

Shape raglans

Keeping patt correct, cast off 2 sts at beg of next 2 rows. 64 [68: 70: 74: 76] sts.
Dec 1 st at each end of next and foll 0 [0: 1: 4: 5] alt rows, then on 2 [2: 2: 0: 0] foll 4th rows. 58 [62: 62: 64: 64] sts.
Work 3 [3: 1: 3: 1] rows, ending after chart row 24 and with RS facing for next row.
Next row (RS): (Work 2 tog) 1 [1: 0: 1: 0] times, moss st 26 [28: 30: 29: 31] sts, work 2 tog, moss st to last 2 [2: 0: 2: 0] sts, (work 2 tog) 1 [1: 0: 1: 0] times. 55 [59: 61: 61: 63] sts.
Now working all sts in moss st, dec 1 st at each end of 4th [4th: 2nd: 4th: 2nd] and every foll 4th row until 43 [45: 45: 45: 47] sts rem.
Work 3 [1: 1: 1: 3] rows, ending with RS facing for next row.

Shape neck

Next row (RS): (Work 2 tog) 1 [0: 0: 0: 1] times, moss st 7 [11: 11: 11: 12] sts and turn, leaving rem sts on a holder.
Work each side of neck separately.
Dec 1 st at neck edge of next 5 [7: 7: 7: 9] rows and at same time dec 1 st at raglan armhole edge of 4th [2nd: 2nd: 2nd: 4th] and 0 [1: 1: 1: 1] foll 4th row, ending with RS facing for next row. 2 sts.
Next row (RS): K2tog and fasten off.
With RS facing, rejoin yarn to rem sts, cast off centre 25 [23: 23: 23: 19] sts, moss st to last 2 [0: 0: 0: 2] sts, (work 2 tog) 1 [0: 0: 0: 1] times.
Complete to match first side, reversing shapings.

SLEEVES

Using 2mm (US 0) needles and yarn B cast on 39 [43: 45: 47: 49] sts.
Work in moss st as given for first leg of back for 9 rows, ending with WS facing for next row.
Row 10 (WS): Moss st 4 [4: 5: 3: 4] sts, inc in next st, (moss st 9 [10: 10: 7: 7] sts, inc in next st) 3 [3: 3: 5: 5] times, moss st to end. 43 [47: 49: 53: 55] sts.
Break off yarn B and join in yarn A.
Change to 2¾mm (US 2) needles.
Beg with a K row, work in st st, shaping sides by inc 1 st at each end of next 3 rows, then on foll alt row.
51 [55: 57: 61: 63] sts.
Work 1 row, ending with RS facing for next row.

Shape raglan

Cast off 2 sts at beg of next 2 rows. 47 [51: 53: 57: 59] sts.
Dec 1 st at each end of next and 1 [1: 1: 0: 0] foll 4th row, then on every foll alt row until 15 sts rem.
Work 1 row, ending with RS facing for next row.

Left sleeve only

Dec 1 st at each end of next row. 13 sts.
Place marker at end of last row to denote front neck point.
Cast off 2 sts at beg of next row. 11 sts.
Dec 1 st at front neck edge of next 6 rows and at same time dec 1 st at back raglan edge of next and foll 2 alt rows. 2 sts.

Right sleeve only

Place marker at end of last row to denote front neck point.
Cast off 2 sts at beg and dec 1 st at end of next row. 12 sts.
Dec 1 st at front neck edge of next 7 rows and at same time dec 1 st at back raglan edge of 2nd and foll 2 alt rows. 2 sts.

Both sleeves

Next row (RS): K2tog and fasten off.

MAKING UP

Press as described on the information page.
Join all raglan seams using back stitch, or mattress stitch if preferred. Sew cast-on edge at base of right back opening edge in place behind left back opening edge.

Back inside leg band

With RS facing, using 2mm (US 0) needles and yarn A, beg and ending at inner edge of cast-off sts at top of moss st, pick up and knit 22 [24: 26: 28: 30] sts up left back inside leg edge, 11 sts from cast-on edge between legs, then 22 [24: 26: 28: 30] sts down right back inside leg edge. 55 [59: 63: 67: 71] sts.
Work in g st for 2 rows, ending with WS facing for next row.
Cast off knitwise (on WS).

Front inside leg band

With RS facing, using 2mm (US 0) needles and yarn A, beg and ending at inner edge of cast-off sts at top of moss st, pick up and knit 22 [24: 26: 28: 30] sts up right front inside leg edge, 11 sts from cast-on edge between legs, then 22 [24: 26: 28: 30] sts down left front inside leg edge. 55 [59: 63: 67: 71] sts.
Row 1 (WS): Knit.
Row 2: K13 [14: 15: 16: 17], *yfwd, K2tog, K12 [13: 14: 15: 16], rep from * twice more.
Work in g st for 2 rows, ending with WS facing for next row.
Cast off knitwise (on WS).
Sew row-end edges of inside leg bands to cast-off sts at top of moss st.

Left collar

Using 2mm (US 0) needles and yarn B cast on 49 [51: 51: 51: 51] sts.
Work in moss st as given for first leg of back for 16 rows, ending with RS facing for next row.
Next row (RS): Moss st to last 8 sts, wrap next st (by slipping next st from left needle to right needle, taking yarn to opposite side of work between needles and then slipping same st back onto left needle - when working back across wrapped sts work the wrapped st and the wrapped loop tog as one st) and turn.
Next row: Moss st to end.
Next row: Moss st to last 15 sts, wrap next st and turn.
Next row: Moss st to end.
Next row: Moss st to last 22 sts, wrap next st and turn.
Next row: Moss st to end.
Next row: Moss st to last 29 sts, wrap next st and turn.
Next row: Moss st to end.
Next row: Moss st to last 36 sts, wrap next st and turn.
Next row: Moss st to end.
Next row: Moss st to last 43 sts, wrap next st and turn.
Next row: Moss st to end.
Work 1 row across all sts.
Next row (WS): P3 [2: 2: 2: 2], P2tog, (P6 [7: 7: 7: 7], P2tog) 5 times, P to end.
Cast off rem 43 [45: 45: 45: 45] sts.

Right collar

Using 2mm (US 0) needles and yarn B cast on 49 [51: 51: 51: 51] sts.
Work in moss st as given for first leg of back for 15 rows, ending with WS facing for next row.
Next row (WS): Moss st to last 8 sts, wrap next st and turn.
Next row: Moss st to end.
Next row: Moss st to last 15 sts, wrap next st and turn.
Next row: Moss st to end.
Next row: Moss st to last 22 sts, wrap next st and turn.
Next row: Moss st to end.
Next row: Moss st to last 29 sts, wrap next st and turn.
Next row: Moss st to end.
Next row: Moss st to last 36 sts, wrap next st and turn.
Next row: Moss st to end.
Next row: Moss st to last 43 sts, wrap next st and turn.
Next row: Moss st to end.
Work 2 rows across all sts.
Next row (WS): P3 [2: 2: 2: 2], P2tog, (P6 [7: 7: 7: 7], P2tog) 5 times, P to end.
Cast off rem 43 [45: 45: 45: 45] sts.
Sew cast-off edges of collars to neck edge, positioning shorter row-end edges so that they meet at centre front and longer row-end edges 2 sts in from back opening edges.
See information page for finishing instructions.

Embroidery

Using photograph and chart as a guide, embroider detail onto chart section using yarn A.

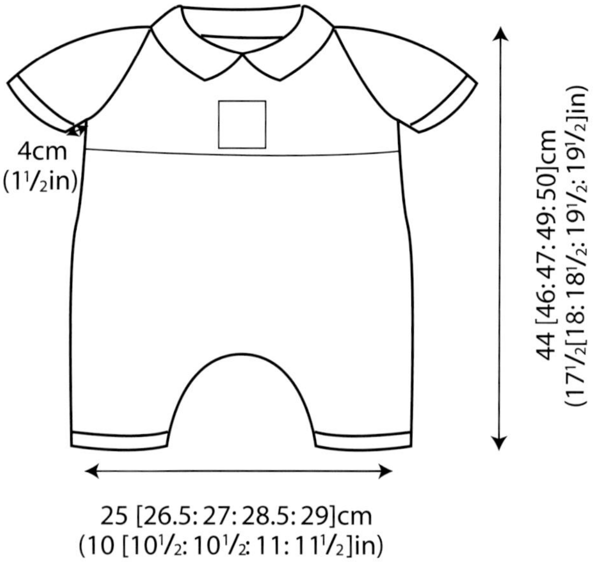

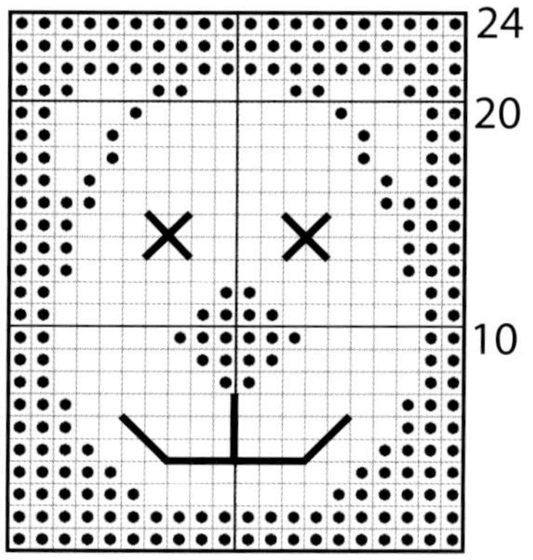

key
- using yarn A, K on RS, P on WS
- using yarn B, K on RS, P on WS
- straight stitches using yarn A

kalli slippers by Lisa Richardson

YARN

To fit age

	0-6	3-9	6-12		months
Rowan Fine Milk Cotton					
	1	1	1	x	50gm

(photographed in either Apple Pips 482 or Humbugs 484)

CROCHET HOOK

2.50mm (no 12) (US C2) crochet hook

TENSION

24 sts and 19 rows to 10 cm measured over htr fabric using 2.50mm (US C2) crochet hook.

UK CROCHET ABBREVIATIONS

ch = chain; **ss** = slip stitch; **dc** = double crochet; **htr** = half treble; **rbdc** = dc worked in the usual way but working around stem of st, inserting hook from back and from right to left; **rbhtr** = htr worked in the usual way but working around stem of st, inserting hook from back and from right to left.

SLIPPERS (both alike)

Sole

Using 2.50mm (US C2) crochet hook make 25 ch.

Round 1 (RS): 1 htr into 3rd ch from hook, 1 htr into each of next 21 ch, 4 htr into last ch, now working back along other side of foundation ch: 1 htr into each of next 21 ch, 2 htr into same ch as htr at beg of round, ss to top of 2 ch at beg of round. 50 sts.

Round 2: 2 ch (counts as first htr), 1 htr into st at base of 2 ch, 1 htr into each of next 23 htr, 2 htr into each of next 2 htr, 1 htr into each of next 23 htr, 2 htr into last htr, ss to top of 2 ch at beg of round. 54 sts.

3-9 and 6-12 months sizes

Round 3: 2 ch (counts as first htr), 1 htr into st at base of 2 ch, 1 htr into each of next 25 htr, 2 htr into each of next 2 htr, 1 htr into each of next 25 htr, 2 htr into last htr, ss to top of 2 ch at beg of round. 58 sts.

6-12 months size

Round 4: 2 ch (counts as first htr), 1 htr into st at base of 2 ch, 1 htr into each of next 27 htr, 2 htr into each of next 2 htr, 1 htr into each of next 27 htr, 2 htr into last htr, ss to top of 2 ch at beg of round. 62 sts.

All sizes

Next round: 1 ss into each of first 5 [6: 7] htr, 1 dc into each of next 4 [5: 6] htr, 1 htr into each of next 17 htr, 2 htr into each of next 2 htr (placing marker between centre 2 of these 4 sts), 1 htr into each of next 17 htr, 1 dc into each of next 4 [5: 6] htr, 1 ss into next htr.

This completes sole.

Shape heel section

Row 1: 1 ch (does NOT count as st), 1 rbdc around stem of htr just worked into, 1 rbhtr around stem of next 8 [10: 12] htr, 1 rbdc around stem of next htr, 1 ss around stem of next 2 htr, turn.

Row 2: 1 ch (does NOT count as st), miss first ss, 1 dc into next ss, 1 htr into each of next 10 [14: 16] sts, 1 dc into next st, 1 ss around stem of next 2 sts of sole, turn.

Rep last row 4 times more.

Fasten off.

This completes heel section.

Shape front section

Rejoin yarn with a ss to 8th [9th: 10th] st before marker at toe, 1 ch, 1 rbdc around stem of next htr, 1 rbhtr around stem of next 12 [14: 16] htr, 1 rbdc around stem of next htr, 1 ss around stem of next htr, turn.

Next row: 1 ch, 1 dc into ss, 1 htr into each of next 12 [14: 16] htr, 1 dc into next dc, 1 ss around stem of next st, turn.

Rep last row 3 times more.

Next row: Miss ss, 1 htr into each st to end, miss 1 htr of sole, 1 ss around stem of each of next 2 sts of sole, turn.

Next row: 1 ch, 1 htr into each htr to end, miss 1 htr of sole, 1 ss around stem of next st, turn.

Rep last row until front section just overlaps heel section.

Fasten off.

MAKING UP

Press as described on the information page.

eric cardi by Marie Wallin

YARN

To fit age

	0-3	3-6	6-9	9-12	12-18	months	2	3	4	years
Rowan Milk Cotton DK										
A Apple Pips 082										
	3	4	4	4	5		5	5	6	x 50gm
B Aniseed 090										
	1	1	1	1	1		1	1	1	x 50gm

NEEDLES

1 pair 3¾mm (no 9) (US 5) needles

BUTTONS – 4 x 00321

TENSION

22 sts and 40 rows to 10 cm measured over g st using 3¾mm (US 5) needles.

BACK

Using 3¾mm (US 5) needles and yarn A cast on 55 [57: 59: 61: 63: 67: 69: 71] sts.
Work in g st until back meas 9 [11: 11: 12: 13: 14: 15: 16] cm, ending with RS facing for next row.

Shape raglan armholes

Cast off 3 sts at beg of next 2 rows.
49 [51: 53: 55: 57: 61: 63: 65] sts.
Next row (RS): P4, K2tog, K to last 6 sts, K2tog tbl, P4.
Next row: Knit.
Next row: P4, K to last 4 sts, P4.
Next row: Knit.
Next row: P4, K to last 4 sts, P4.
Next row: Knit.
Last 6 rows set the sts and raglan armhole shaping.
Cont as set, dec 1 st at each end of next and 6 [6: 6: 4: 4: 2: 2: 0] foll 6th rows, then on 3 [3: 4: 7: 8: 11: 12: 15] foll 4th rows.
27 [29: 29: 29: 29: 31: 31: 31] sts.
Work 3 rows, ending with RS facing for next row.
Cast off.

RIGHT FRONT

Using 3¾mm (US 5) needles and yarn A cast on 31 [32: 33: 34: 35: 37: 38: 39] sts.
Work in g st until right front matches back to beg of raglan armhole shaping, ending with WS facing for next row.

Shape raglan armholes

Cast off 3 sts at beg of next row. 28 [29: 30: 31: 32: 34: 35: 36] sts.
Working all raglan shaping as given for back, dec 1 st at raglan armhole edge of next and 3 [3: 4: 4: 4: 3: 3: 1] foll 6th rows, then on 0 [0: 0: 0: 0: 2: 3: 5] foll 4th rows. 24 [25: 25: 26: 27: 28: 28: 29] sts.
Work 5 [3: 1: 1: 3: 1: 1: 3] rows, ending with RS facing for next row.

Shape front slope

Keeping raglan shaping correct as set, dec 1 st at front slope edge of next 9 [9: 9: 9: 7: 9: 9: 7] rows, then on foll 6 [7: 7: 7: 9: 8: 8: 10] alt rows and at same time dec 1 st at raglan armhole edge of next [3rd: 5th: 5th: 3rd: 3rd: 3rd: next] row and 3 [3: 2: 0: 0: 0: 0: 0] foll 6th rows, then on 0 [0: 1: 4: 5: 5: 5: 6] foll 4th rows. 5 sts.
Work 1 row.
Next row (RS): P3tog, P2. 3 sts.
Next row: K3.
Next row: P2tog, P1.
Next row:K2.
Next row (RS): P2tog and fasten off.
Mark positions for 4 buttons along right front opening edge - first to come in row 17, last to come 1.5 cm below beg of front slope shaping, and rem 2 buttons evenly spaced between.

LEFT FRONT

Using 3¾mm (US 5) needles and yarn A cast on 31 [32: 33: 34: 35: 37: 38: 39] sts.
Work in g st for 16 rows, ending with RS facing for next row.
Row 17 (buttonhole row) (RS): K to last 4 sts, yfwd (to make a buttonhole), K2tog, K2.
Working a further 3 buttonholes in this way to correspond with positions marked for buttons, complete to match right front, reversing shapings.

SLEEVES

Using 3¾mm (US 5) needles and yarn A cast on 27 [29: 29: 31: 31: 33: 33: 35] sts.
Work in g st, shaping sides by inc 1 st at each end of

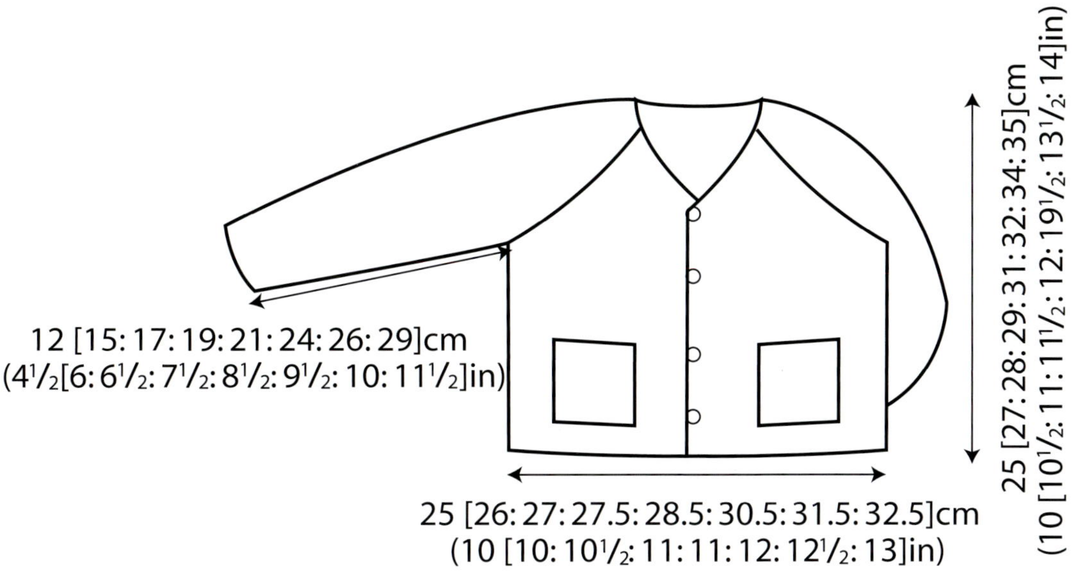

3rd [5th: 5th: 5th: 5th: 7th: 7th: 7th] and every foll 4th [6th: 6th: 6th: 6th: 8th: 8th: 8th] row to 33 [37: 37: 35: 35: 43: 49: 39] sts, then on every foll 6th [8th: 8th: 8th: 8th: 10th: 10th: 10th] row until there are 41 [43: 45: 47: 49: 51: 53: 55] sts.
Cont straight until sleeve meas 12 [15: 17: 19: 21: 24: 26: 29] cm, ending with RS facing for next row.

Shape raglan

Cast off 3 sts at beg of next 2 rows. 35 [37: 39: 41: 43: 45: 47: 49] sts.
Working all raglan shaping as given for back, dec 1 st at each end of next and foll 1 [3: 3: 5: 5: 7: 7: 9] alt rows, then on every foll 4th row until 11 sts rem.
Work 3 rows, ending with RS facing for next row.
Next row (RS): P4, sl 1, K2tog, psso, P4. 9 sts.
Work 3 rows, ending with RS facing for next row.

Left sleeve only

Place marker at beg of last row to denote top of left front raglan edge.
Next row (RS): P4, P2tog, P1, P2tog. 7 sts.
Next row: K2tog, K5.
Next row: P4, P2tog. 5 sts.
Next row: K5.
Next row: P2, P3tog. 3 sts.
Next row: K3.
Next row: P1, P2tog.

Right sleeve only

Place marker at end of last row to denote top of right front raglan edge.
Next row (RS): P2tog, P1, P2tog, P4. 7 sts.
Next row: K5, K2tog.
Next row: P2tog, P4. 5 sts.
Next row: K5.
Next row: P3tog, P2. 3 sts.
Next row: K3.
Next row: P2tog, P1.

Both sleeves

Next row (WS): K2.
Next row: P2tog and fasten off.

MAKING UP

Press as described on the information page.

Pockets (make 2)

Using 3¾mm (US 5) needles and yarn A cast on 16 [16: 17: 17: 18: 18: 19: 19] sts.
Work in g st for 7 [7: 8: 8: 8: 8: 9: 9] cm, ending with RS facing for next row.
Cast off.
See information page for finishing instructions.
Using yarn B and using photograph as a guide, work blanket stitch around entire lower, front opening, neck and cuff edges, and across top of pockets. Sew pockets onto fronts as in photograph.

edith shrug by Marie Wallin

YARN

To fit age	9-18 months	2-3 years
Rowan Fine Milk Cotton		
	1	2 x 50gm

(photographed in Sherbert 480)

NEEDLES

2.50mm (no 12) (US C2) crochet hook

TENSION

One motif measures 5 cm in diameter using 2.50mm (US C2) crochet hook.

UK CROCHET ABBREVIATIONS

ch = chain; **ss** = slip stitch; **dc** = double crochet; **tr** = treble; **tr2tog** = (yoh and insert hook as indicated, yoh and draw loop through, yoh and draw through 2 loops) twice, yoh and draw through all 3 loops; **tr3tog** = (yoh and insert hook as indicated, yoh and draw loop through, yoh and draw through 2 loops) 3 times, yoh and draw through all 4 loops; **sp** = space.

MOTIFS (make 37 [39])
Using 2.50mm (US C2) crochet hook, make 8 ch and join with a ss to form a ring.
Round 1 (RS): 1 ch (does NOT count as st), 16 dc into ring, ss to first dc. 16 sts.
Round 2: 3 ch (does NOT count as st), tr2tog into st at base of 3 ch, *3 ch, miss 1 dc**, tr3tog into next dc, rep from * to end, ending last rep at **, ss to top of tr2tog at beg of round.
Round 3: 6 ch (counts as 1 tr and 3 ch), miss st at base of 3 ch, *1 dc into next ch sp, 3 ch**, 1 tr into next tr3tog, 3 ch, rep from * to end, ending last rep at **, ss to 3rd of 6 ch at beg of round.
Fasten off.

TIES (make 2)
Using 2.50mm (US C2) crochet hook, make 40 ch.
Row 1 (RS): 1 dc into 2nd ch from hook, 1 dc into each ch to end.
Fasten off.

MAKING UP
Press as described on the information page.
Following appropriate diagram, sew motifs together where indicated (by lines between motifs) to form shape shown, then join shoulder seams (indicated by dashed lines) to complete shrug. Attach ties to centre front motifs as in photograph.

9 - 18 months

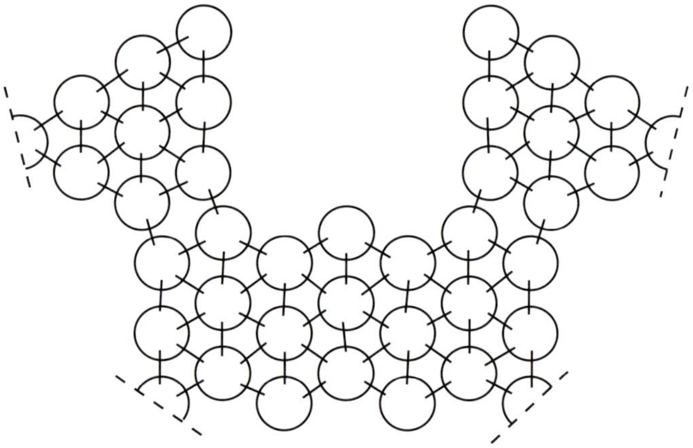

2 - 3 years

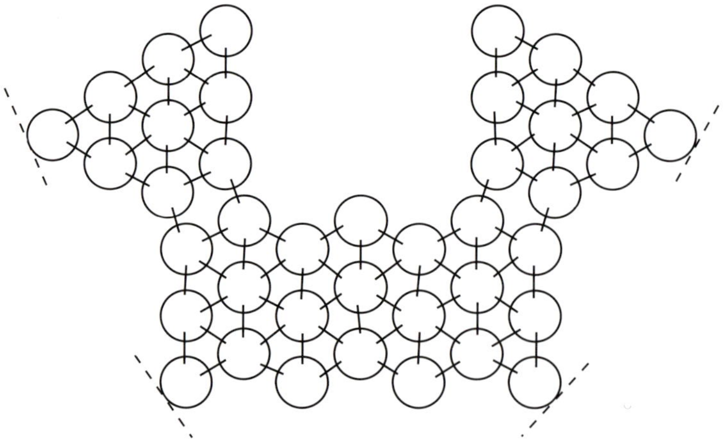

la la teddy by Lisa Richardson

YARN
Rowan Milk Cotton DK
1 x 50gm
Small amount of same yarn in contrast colour for neck tie and embroidery (photographed in Humbugs 084 with embroidery in Scented Satin 088)

NEEDLES
1 pair 3¼mm (no 10) (US 3) needles

EXTRAS - washable toy filling

TENSION
26 sts and 34 rows to 10 cm measured over st st using 3¼mm (US 3) needles.

FINISHED SIZE
Completed toy is approx 28 cm (11 ins) tall.

BACK and FRONT (both alike)

First leg
Using 3¼mm (US 3) needles cast on 7 sts.
Beg with a K row, work in st st throughout as folls:
Work 1 row, ending with WS facing for next row.
Inc 1 st at each end of next 2 rows, then at beg of foll row. 12 sts.
Work 2 rows, ending with RS facing for next row.
Inc 1 st at beg of next and 4 foll 4th rows and at same time dec 1 st at end of 7th and 2 foll 4th rows. 14 sts.
Inc 1 st at end of next row, ending with RS facing for next row. 15 sts.
Break yarn and leave sts on a holder.

Second leg
Using 3¼mm (US 3) needles cast on 7 sts.
Beg with a K row, work in st st throughout as folls:
Work 1 row, ending with WS facing for next row.
Inc 1 st at each end of next 2 rows, then at end of foll row. 12 sts.
Work 2 rows, ending with RS facing for next row.
Inc 1 st at end of next and 4 foll 4th rows and at same time dec 1 st at beg of 7th and 2 foll 4th rows. 14 sts.
Inc 1 st at beg of next row, ending with RS facing for next row. 15 sts.

Join legs
Row 25 (RS): Work across sts of second leg as folls: K2tog, K12, inc in last st, now work across sts of first leg as folls: inc in first st, K12, K2tog. 30 sts.
Work 3 rows, ending with RS facing for next row.
Dec 1 st at each end of next and foll 4th row. 26 sts.
Work 15 rows, ending with RS facing for next row.

Shape arms
Cast on 7 sts at beg of next 2 rows, then 10 sts at beg of foll 2 rows. 60 sts.
Inc 1 st at each end of next 2 rows. 64 sts.
Work 6 rows.
Dec 1 st at each end of next 2 rows. 60 sts.
Cast off 12 sts at beg of next 2 rows, then 10 sts at beg of foll 2 rows. 16 sts.
Work 2 rows, ending with RS facing for next row.

Shape head
Inc 1 st at each end of next 4 rows, then on foll alt row, then on foll 4th row. 28 sts.
Work 5 rows, ending with WS facing for next row.
Inc 1 st at each end of next 4 rows. 36 sts.
Work 4 rows, ending with WS facing for next row.

Shape top of first ear
Next row (WS): P9, P2tog and turn.
Work on these 10 sts only for top of first ear.
Dec 1 st at each end of next 3 rows, ending with WS facing for next row.
Cast off rem 4 sts.

Shape top of head
With WS facing, rejoin yarn to rem sts and cont as folls:
Next row (WS): P2tog, P10, P2tog and turn.
Work on these 12 sts only for top of head.
Dec 1 st at each end of next 2 rows, ending with RS facing for next row.
Cast off rem 8 sts.

Shape top of second ear
With WS facing, rejoin yarn to rem sts and cont as folls:
Next row (WS): P2tog, P9.
Work on these 10 sts only for top of second ear.
Dec 1 st at each end of next 3 rows, ending with WS facing for next row.
Cast off rem 4 sts.

MAKING UP

Press as described on the information page.
Join back to front along entire outer edges, leaving an opening to insert toy filling. Insert toy filling and sew opening closed. Using photograph as a guide and contrast yarn, embroider face onto front, and a "V" onto each ear. Using contrast yarn, make a plait approx 40 cm long, knotting ends to form tiny tassels. Tie plait in a bow around neck.

faye cardi by Marie Wallin

YARN

To fit age									
	0-3	3-6	6-9	9-12	12-18	months	2	3	4 years
Rowan Fine Milk Cotton									
	2	2	3	3	3		3	3	4 x 50gm

Small amount of Milk Cotton in contrast colour for embroidery
(photographed in Shrimps 483 with embroidery in Milk Cotton DK, Bubble Gum 086)

NEEDLES
1 pair 2mm (no 14) (US 0) needles
1 pair 2¾mm (no 12) (US 2) needles

EXTRAS - tiny amount of washable toy filling

TENSION
30 sts and 38 rows to 10 cm measured over st st using 2 ¾mm (US 2) needles.

BACK

Using 2¾mm (US 2) needles cast on 75 [79: 81: 85: 87: 91: 93: 97] sts.
Beg with a K row, work in st st for 12 [18: 18: 26: 26: 34: 34: 42] rows, ending with RS facing for next row.
(Back should meas 3 [5: 5: 7: 7: 9: 9: 11] cm.)

Shape armholes
Cast off 3 sts at beg of next 2 rows. 69 [73: 75: 79: 81: 85: 87: 91] sts.
Dec 1 st at each end of next 1 [3: 3: 3: 3: 5: 5: 5] rows, then on foll 3 [3: 3: 4: 4: 4: 4: 5] alt rows. 61 [61: 63: 65: 67: 67: 69: 71] sts.
Work 27 [25: 29: 27: 31: 29: 33: 31] rows, ending with RS facing for next row. (Armhole should meas 10 [10: 11: 11: 12: 12: 13: 13] cm.)

Shape back neck and shoulder
Cast off 4 [4: 4: 5: 5: 5: 5: 5] sts at beg of next 2 rows.
53 [53: 55: 55: 57: 57: 59: 61] sts.
Next row (RS): Cast off 4 [4: 4: 5: 5: 5: 5: 5] sts, K until there are 8 [7: 8: 7: 8: 7: 8: 8] sts on right needle and turn, leaving rem sts on a holder.
Work each side of neck separately.
Cast off 3 sts at beg of next row.
Cast off rem 5 [4: 5: 4: 5: 4: 5: 5] sts.
With RS facing, rejoin yarn to rem sts, cast off centre 29 [31: 31: 31: 31: 33: 33: 35] sts, K to end.
Complete to match first side, reversing shapings.

LEFT FRONT

Using 2¾mm (US 2) needles cast on 19 [20: 19: 18: 19: 18: 17: 17] sts.
Beg with a K row, work in st st as folls:
Work 1 row, ending with WS facing for next row.
Inc 1 st at beg of next row and at same edge on foll 10 [11: 13: 13: 15: 15: 17: 17] rows, then on foll 0 [2: 1: 5: 4: 7: 6: 8] alt rows, then on 0 [0: 0: 0: 0: 0: 0: 1] foll 4th row. 30 [34: 34: 37: 39: 41: 41: 44] sts.
Work 0 [1: 1: 1: 1: 3: 3: 3] rows, ending with RS facing for next row.

Shape armhole
Cast off 3 sts at beg and inc 1 [1: 1: 1: 0: 1: 1: 1] st at end of next row. 28 [32: 32: 35: 36: 39: 39: 42] sts.
Work 1 row.
Dec 1 st at armhole edge of next 1 [3: 3: 3: 3: 5: 5: 5] rows, then on foll 3 [3: 3: 4: 4: 4: 4: 5] alt rows and at same time inc 1 st at front opening edge of next [next: next: next: next: 3rd: 3rd: 3rd] and foll 3 [1: 1: 0: 0: 0: 0: 0] alt rows, then on 0 [1: 1: 2: 1: 0: 1: 0] foll 4th rows, then on 0 [0: 0: 0: 1: 1: 1: 2] foll 6th rows.
28 [29: 29: 31: 32: 32: 33: 35] sts.
Inc 1 st at front opening edge only on 4th [4th: 2nd: 4th: 6th: 2nd: 6th: 0] and 1 [0: 1: 0: 0: 0: 0: 0] foll 6th row.
30 [30: 31: 32: 33: 33: 34: 35] sts.
Work 4 [6: 6: 8: 8: 10: 10: 12] rows, ending with WS facing for next row.

Shape neck
Cast off 9 [9: 9: 9: 8: 9: 9: 9] sts at beg of next row.
21 [21: 22: 23: 25: 24: 25: 26] sts.
Dec 1 st at neck edge of next 7 rows, then on foll 1 [2: 2: 2: 3: 3: 3: 4] alt rows. 13 [12: 13: 14: 15: 14: 15: 15] sts.
Work 3 rows, ending with RS facing for next row.

Shape shoulder
Cast off 4 [4: 4: 5: 5: 5: 5: 5] sts at beg of next and foll alt row.
Work 1 row.
Cast off rem 5 [4: 5: 4: 5: 4: 5: 5] sts.

RIGHT FRONT

Using 2¾mm (US 2) needles cast on 19 [20: 19: 18: 19: 18: 17: 17] sts.
Beg with a K row, work in st st as folls:
Work 1 row, ending with WS facing for next row.
Inc 1 st at end of next row and at same edge on foll 10 [11: 13: 13:

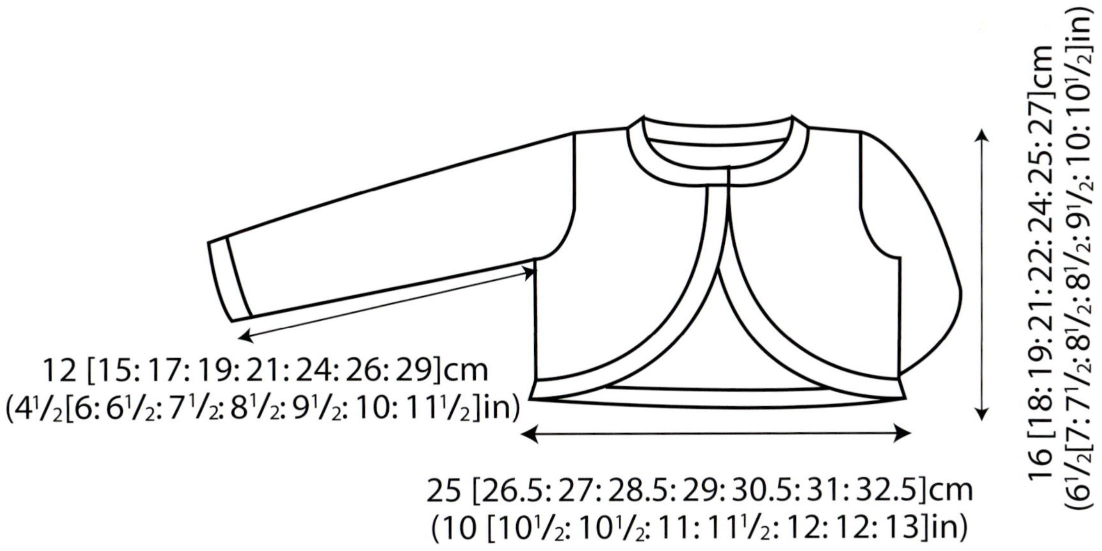

15: 15: 17: 17] rows, then on foll 0 [2: 1: 5: 4: 7: 6: 8] alt rows, then on 0 [0: 0: 0: 0: 0: 0: 1] foll 4th row. 30 [34: 34: 37: 39: 41: 41: 44] sts.
Complete to match left front, reversing shapings.

SLEEVES

Using 2¾mm (US 2) needles cast on 39 [43: 43: 45: 45: 49: 49: 51] sts.
Beg with a K row, work in st st, shaping sides by inc 1 st at each end of 3rd [5th: 5th: 5th: 5th: 5th: 5th: 7th] and every foll alt [4th: 4th: 4th: 4th: 4th: 6th: 6th] row to 49 [59: 57: 61: 59: 53: 75: 75] sts, then on every foll 4th [6th: 6th: 6th: 6th: 6th: -: 8th] row until there are 57 [61: 63: 67: 69: 73: -: 79] sts.
Cont straight until sleeve meas 10 [13: 15: 17: 19: 22: 24: 27] cm, ending with RS facing for next row.

Shape top

Cast off 3 [3: 3: 3: 2: 3: 2: 2] sts at beg of next 10 [8: 14: 12: 2: 16: 4: 2] rows, then 4 [4: 0: 4: 3: 0: 3: 3] sts at beg of foll 2 [4: 0: 2: 14: 0: 14: 16] rows.
Cast off rem 19 [21: 21: 23: 23: 25: 25: 27] sts.

MAKING UP

Press as described on the information page.
Join both shoulder seams using back stitch, or mattress stitch if preferred.

Cuff edgings (both alike)

Using 2mm (US 0) needles cast on 7 sts.
Row 1 (RS): K1, K2tog, (yfwd) twice, K2tog, (yfwd) twice, K2. 9 sts.
Row 2: K3, (P1, K2) twice.
Row 3: K1, K2tog, (yfwd) twice, K2tog, K4.
Row 4: Cast off 2 sts (one st on right needle), K3, P1, K2. 7 sts.
These 4 rows form patt.
Cont in patt until edging strip fits neatly across cast-on edge of sleeve, ending after patt row 4 and with RS facing for next row.
Cast off.
Slip stitch cuff edging in place.
Join side and cuff edging seams.

Front opening and hem edging

Work as given for cuff edging, making a strip that fits neatly around entire front opening and lower (cast-on) edges of fronts and back, beg and ending at neck shaping and easing edging around curved edges so that it lays flat.
Slip stitch edging in place.

Neck edging

Work as given for cuff edging, making a strip that fits neatly around entire neck edge, beg and ending at outer edge of front edging and easing edging around curves so that it lays flat.
Slip stitch edging in place.
See information page for finishing instructions, setting in sleeves using the shallow set-in method.

Button

Using 2mm (US 0) needles cast on 14 sts.
Work in g st for 4 rows, ending with RS facing for next row.
Row 5 (RS): (K2tog) 7 times.
Break yarn and thread through rem 7 sts. Pull up tight and fasten off securely. Sew row-end edges together. Run a gathering thread around cast-on edge and insert a little toy filling. Pull up gathering thread and fasten off securely. Using photograph as a guide, and one "hole" of front edging as a buttonhole, sew on button.

Embroidery

Using photograph as a guide, embroider cross stitch hearts and kisses onto fronts using contrast yarn. The contrast embroidery DK yarn is split in order to acheive a finer finish.

freddie coat by Marie Wallin

YARN

To fit age

	0-3	3-6	6-9	9-12	12-18	months	2		years
Rowan Milk Cotton DK									
A Scented Satin 088									
	5	6	7	7	8		8	x	50gm
B Humbugs 084									
	1	1	1	1	1		1	x	50gm

NEEDLES

1 pair 3¼mm (no 10) (US 3) needles, 1 pair 3¾mm (no 9) (US 5) needles & 3.00mm (no 11) (US D3) crochet hook

EXTRAS - 4 x 00406 buttons and 4 stud fasteners

TENSION

22 sts and 30 rows to 10 cm measured over st st using 3¾mm (US 5) needles.
22 sts and 40 rows to 10 cm measured over g st using 3¼mm (US 3) needles.

UK CROCHET ABBREVIATIONS

ch = chain; **dc** = double crochet.

BACK

Using 3¼mm (US 3) needles and yarn B cast on 110 [114: 118: 122: 126: 130] sts.
Work in g st for 4 rows, ending with RS facing for next row.
Break off yarn B and join in yarn A.
Change to 3¾mm (US 5) needles.
Beg with a K row, work in st st until back meas 25 [28: 29: 31: 33: 35] cm, ending with RS facing for next row.
Change to 3¼mm (US 3) needles.
Next row (RS): K1, *sl 1, K1, psso, rep from * to last st, K1. 56 [58: 60: 62: 64: 66] sts.
Next row: Purl.
Work in g st until back meas 27 [30: 31: 33: 35: 37] cm, ending with RS facing for next row.

Shape armholes

Cast off 2 sts at beg of next 2 rows. 52 [54: 56: 58: 60: 62] sts.
Dec 1 st at each end of next 1 [1: 3: 3: 3: 3] rows, then on foll 2 [2: 1: 1: 2: 2] alt rows. 46 [48: 48: 50: 50: 52] sts.
Cont straight until armhole meas 10 [10: 11: 11: 12: 12] cm, ending with RS facing for next row.

Shape shoulders and back neck

Cast off 3 [3: 3: 4: 4: 4] sts at beg of next 2 rows. 40 [42: 42: 42: 42: 44] sts.
Next row (RS): Cast off 3 [3: 3: 4: 4: 4] sts, K until there are 7 [7: 7: 6: 6: 6] sts on right needle and turn, leaving rem sts on a holder.
Work each side of neck separately.
Cast off 3 sts at beg of next row.
Cast off rem 4 [4: 4: 3: 3: 3] sts.
With RS facing, rejoin yarn to rem sts, cast off centre 20 [22: 22: 22: 22: 24] sts, K to end.
Complete to match first side, reversing shapings.

LEFT FRONT

Using 3¼mm (US 3) needles and yarn B cast on 76 [78: 80: 82: 84: 86] sts.
Work in g st for 4 rows, ending with RS facing for next row.
Break off yarn B and join in yarn A.
Change to 3¾mm (US 5) needles.
Beg with a K row, work in st st until left front meas 25 [28: 29: 31: 33: 35] cm, ending with RS facing for next row.
Change to 3¼mm (US 3) needles.
Next row (RS): K1, *sl 1, K1, psso, rep from * to last st, K1. 39 [40: 41: 42: 43: 44] sts.
Next row: Purl.
Work in g st until left front matches back to beg of armhole shaping, ending with RS facing for next row.

Shape armhole

Cast off 2 sts at beg of next row. 37 [38: 39: 40: 41: 42] sts.
Work 1 row.
Dec 1 st at armhole edge of next 1 [1: 3: 3: 3: 3] rows, then on foll 2 [2: 1: 1: 2: 2] alt rows. 34 [35: 35: 36: 36: 37] sts.
Cont straight until 9 [11: 11: 11: 13: 13] rows less have been worked than on back to beg of shoulder shaping, ending with WS facing for next row.

Shape neck

Cast off 18 [18: 18: 18: 17: 18] sts at beg of next row. 16 [17: 17: 18: 19: 19] sts.
Dec 1 st at neck edge of next 5 rows, then on foll 1 [2: 2: 2: 3: 3] alt rows. 10 [10: 10: 11: 11: 11] sts.
Work 1 row, ending with RS facing for next row.

Shape shoulder

Cast off 3 [3: 3: 4: 4: 4] sts at beg of next and foll alt row.
Work 1 row.

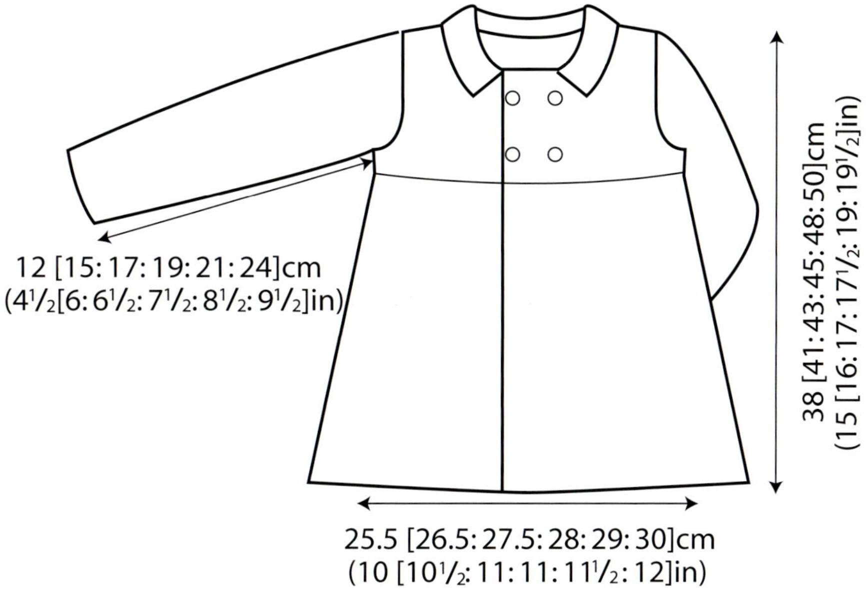

Cast off rem 4 [4: 4: 3: 3: 3] sts.

RIGHT FRONT

Work to match left front, reversing shapings.

SLEEVES

Using 3¼mm (US 3) needles and yarn B cast on 29 [31: 31: 33: 33: 35] sts.
Work in g st for 4 rows, ending with RS facing for next row.
Break off yarn B and join in yarn A.
Change to 3¾mm (US 5) needles.
Beg with a K row, work in st st, shaping sides by inc 1 st at each end of next [3rd: 3rd: 3rd: 3rd: 5th] and every foll alt [4th: 4th: 4th: 4th: 6th] row to 37 [39: 45: 39: 45: 49] sts, then on every foll 4th [6th: 6th: 6th: 6th: 8th] row until there are 45 [45: 49: 49: 53: 53] sts.
Cont straight until sleeve meas 12 [15: 17: 19: 21: 24] cm, ending with RS facing for next row.

Shape top

Cast off 2 sts at beg of next 2 rows. 41 [41: 45: 45: 49: 49] sts.
Dec 1 st at each end of next 3 rows, then on every foll alt row until 33 sts rem, then on foll 5 rows, ending with RS facing for next row. 23 sts.
Cast off 3 sts at beg of next 2 rows.
Cast off rem 17 sts.

MAKING UP

Press as described on the information page.
Join both shoulder seams using back stitch, or mattress stitch if preferred.

Collar

Using 3¼mm (US 3) needles and yarn B cast on 70 [78: 78: 78: 82: 86] sts.
Work in g st for 4 rows, ending with RS facing for next row.
Break off yarn B and join in yarn A.
Cont in g st until collar meas 4 cm, ending with RS facing for next row.
Cast off 2 [3: 3: 3: 3: 3] sts at beg of next 2 [8: 8: 8: 4: 2] rows, then 3 [4: 4: 4: 4: 4] sts at beg of foll 10 [4: 4: 4: 8: 10] rows.
Cast off rem 36 [38: 38: 38: 38: 40] sts.
Positioning row-end edges of collar 14 sts in from front opening edges, sew shaped cast-off edge of collar to neck edge.

Front borders (both alike)

With RS facing, using 3.00mm (US D3) crochet hook and yarn B, attach yarn at one end of one front opening edge, 1 ch (does NOT count as st), work 1 row of dc evenly along entire front opening edge, turn.
Next row: 1 ch (does NOT count as st), 1 dc into each dc to end, turn.
Rep last row once more.
Fasten off.
See information page for finishing instructions, setting in sleeves using the set-in method. Lay one front over other front (left over right for a girl, or right over left for a boy) so that they overlap by 22 knitted sts. Attach 4 stud fasteners to secure fronts, attaching buttons on outer layer at stud positions as in photograph.

tabitha coat by Marie Wallin

YARN

To fit age	0-3	3-6	6-9	9-12	12-18	months	2	years
Rowan Milk Cotton DK								
A Bon Bon 092	5	6	7	7	8		8	x 50gm
B Aniseed 090	1	1	1	1	1		1	x 50gm
C Fruit Salad 089	1	1	1	1	1		1	x 50gm
D Scented Satin 088	1	1	1	1	1		1	x 50gm
E Bubble Gum 086	1	1	1	1	1		1	x 50gm

NEEDLES

1 pair 3¼mm (no 10) (US 3) needles, 1 pair 3¾mm (no 9) (US 5) needles & 3.00mm (no 11) (US D3) crochet hook

EXTRAS - 4 stud fasteners

TENSION

22 sts and 30 rows to 10 cm measured over st st using 3¾mm (US 5) needles.
22 sts and 40 rows to 10 cm measured over g st using 3¼mm (US 3) needles.

UK CROCHET ABBREVIATIONS

ch = chain; **dc** = double crochet; **ss** = slip stitch; **tr2tog** = *yarn over hook and insert hook into next st, yarn over hook and draw loop through, yarn over hook and draw through 2 loops, rep from * once more, yarn over hook and draw through all 3 loops.

BACK, FRONTS and SLEEVES

Work as given for Freddie but using yarn A throughout.

MAKING UP

Press as described on the information page.
Join both shoulder seams using back stitch, or mattress stitch if preferred.
Collar and Front borders (both alike)
Work as given for Freddie but using yarn A throughout.
Flowers (make 4)
Using 3.00mm (US D3) crochet hook and contrast yarn, make 6 ch and join with a ss to form a ring.
Round 1: 1 ch (does NOT count as st), 15 dc into ring, ss to first dc.
Round 2: *3 ch, miss st at base of 3 ch, tr2tog over next 2 dc, 3 ch, 1 ss into next dc, rep from * 4 times more.
Fasten off.
Make a further 3 flowers in this way, using colours as shown in photograph.
See information page for finishing instructions, setting in sleeves using the set-in method. Lay one front over other front (left over right for a girl, or right over left for a boy) so that they overlap by 22 knitted sts. Attach 4 stud fasteners to secure fronts, attaching flowers on outer layer at stud positions. Embroider large french knots at centre of flower to form flower centre.

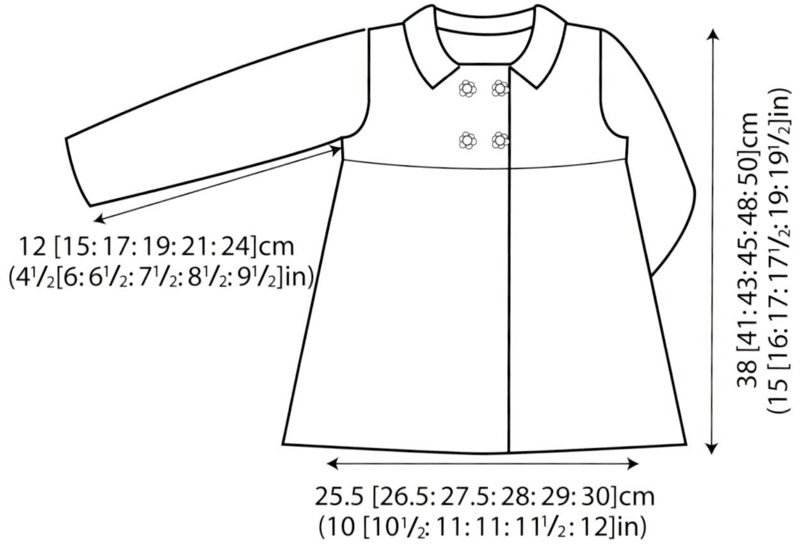

margo jumper by Marie Wallin

YARN

To fit age

	0-3	3-6	6-9	9-12	12-18	months	2	3	4	years
Rowan Milk Cotton DK										
A Scented Satin 088	1	1	1	1	1		2	2	2	x 50gm
B Tutti Fruitti 087	1	1	1	1	1		1	2	2	x 50gm
C Fruit Salad 089	1	1	1	2	2		2	2	2	x 50gm
D Shrimps 083	1	1	1	1	1		1	2	2	x 50gm
E Bubble Gum 086	1	1	1	1	1		1	1	2	x 50gm

NEEDLES

1 pair 3¾mm (no 9) (US 5) needles & 3.50mm (no 9) (US E4) crochet hook

BUTTONS – 3 x 00333

TENSION

23 sts and 29 rows to 10 cm measured over patt using 3¾mm (US 5) needles.

CROCHET ABBREVIATIONS

ch = chain; **ss** = slip stitch; **dc** = double crochet; **tr** = treble.

BACK

Using 3¾mm (US 5) needles and yarn A cast on 59 [61: 63: 67: 69: 71: 73: 75] sts.

Row 1 (RS): K1, *yfwd, K2tog, rep from * to end.

Row 2: P1, *K1, P1, rep from * to end.

Break off yarn A and join in yarn B.

Row 3: K1, *P1, K1, rep from * to end.

Row 4: As row 2.

Beg and ending rows as indicated and repeating the 66 row patt rep throughout, work in patt from chart for body as folls:

Work straight until back meas 16 [18: 18: 20: 20: 22: 22: 24] cm, ending with RS facing for next row.

Shape armholes

Keeping patt correct, cast off 2 [2: 2: 2: 2: 3: 3: 3] sts at beg of next 2 rows. 55 [57: 59: 63: 65: 65: 67: 69] sts.

(Note: No shaping is shown on chart.)

Dec 1 st at each end of next 1 [1: 1: 3: 3: 3: 3: 3] rows, then on foll 0 [1: 1: 1: 1: 1: 1: 1] alt rows. 53 [53: 55: 55: 57: 57: 59: 61] sts.**

Cont straight until armhole meas 11 [11: 12: 12: 13: 13: 14: 14] cm, ending with RS facing for next row.

Shape back neck

Next row (RS): Patt 13 [12: 13: 13: 14: 13: 14: 14] sts and turn, leaving rem sts on a holder.

Work each side of neck separately.

Dec 1 st at neck edge of next row. 12 [11: 12: 12: 13: 12: 13: 13] sts.

Place markers at both ends of last row (to denote shoulder line).

Shape right front shoulder panel

Work 6 rows, ending with RS facing for next row.

Inc 1 st at neck edge of next and foll 1 [1: 1: 1: 2: 2: 2: 3] alt rows, then on foll row, taking inc sts into patt and ending with RS facing for next row.

Cast off all 15 [14: 15: 15: 17: 16: 17: 18] sts.

With RS facing, rejoin appropriate yarn to rem sts, cast off centre 27 [29: 29: 29: 29: 31: 31: 33] sts, patt to end.

Dec 1 st at neck edge of next row.

Cast off rem 12 [11: 12: 12: 13: 12: 13: 13] sts.

FRONT

Work as given for back to **.

Cont straight until 12 [12: 12: 12: 14: 14: 14: 16] rows less have been worked than on back to shoulder, ending with RS facing for next row.

Shape neck

Next row (RS): Patt 21 [20: 21: 21: 23: 22: 23: 24] sts and turn, leaving rem sts on a holder.

Work each side of neck separately.

Keeping patt correct, cast off 6 sts at beg of next row. 15 [14: 15: 15: 17: 16: 17: 18] sts.

Dec 1 st at neck edge of next 2 rows, then on foll 1 [1: 1: 1: 2: 2: 2: 3] alt rows. 12 [11: 12: 12: 13: 12: 13: 13] sts.

Work 6 rows, ending with RS facing for next row.

Cast off.

With RS facing, rejoin yarn to rem sts, cast off centre 11 [13: 13: 13: 11: 13: 13: 13] sts, patt to end.

Work 1 row.

Cast off all sts, placing marker after 6th cast-off st.

SLEEVES

Using 3¾mm (US 5) needles and yarn A cast on 27 [29: 33: 35: 37: 39: 39: 41] sts.

Work rows 1 to 4 as given for back, ending with RS facing for next row.

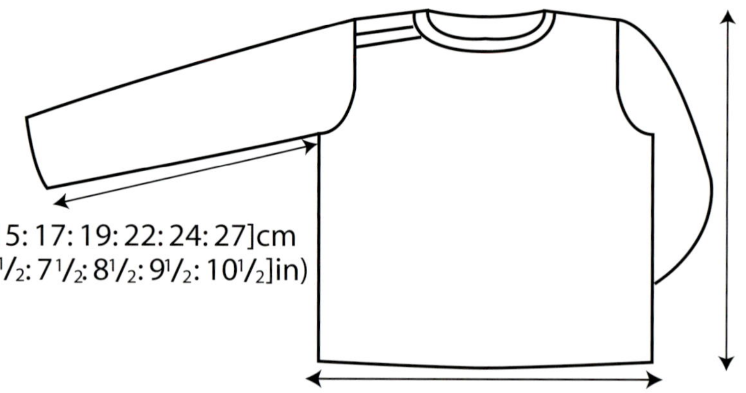

Beg and ending rows as indicated, work in patt from chart as folls: Inc 1 st at each end of next [next: next: 3rd: 3rd: 5th: 3rd: 5th] and foll 4 [0: 0: 0: 0: 0: 0: 0] rows, then on foll 5 [4: 2: 0: 0: 0: 0: 0] alt rows, then on 0 [4: 6: 5: 6: 0: 2: 0] foll 4th rows, then on 0 [0: 0: 2: 2: 7: 7: 4] foll 6th rows, then on 0 [0: 0: 0: 0: 0: 0: 4] foll 8th rows, taking inc sts into patt. 47 [47: 51: 51: 55: 55: 59: 59] sts.
Cont straight until sleeve meas 10 [13: 15: 17: 19: 22: 24: 27] cm, ending with RS facing for next row.

Shape top

Keeping patt correct, cast off 2 [2: 2: 2: 2: 3: 3: 3] sts at beg of next 2 rows. 43 [43: 47: 47: 51: 49: 53: 53] sts.
Dec 1 st at each end of next 3 rows, then on foll 1 [1: 2: 2: 3: 3: 4: 4] alt rows, then on foll 3 rows, ending with RS facing for next row. 29 [29: 31: 31: 33: 31: 33: 33] sts.
Cast off 7 sts at beg of next 2 rows.
Cast off rem 15 [15: 17: 17: 19: 17: 19: 19] sts.

MAKING UP

Press as described on the information page.
Join left shoulder seam using back stitch, or mattress stitch if preferred.

Neck and right shoulder opening trim

With WS facing, using 3.50mm (US E4) crochet hook and yarn B, attach yarn at armhole edge of right front "shoulder" cast-off edge, 1 ch (does NOT count as st), work in dc across cast-off edge to marker, now cont in dc across front neck edge, up left front slope, across back neck, down right front slope of right shoulder panel, then across cast-off edge of shoulder panel ending at armhole edge, ensuring number of dc worked after marker is a multiple of 5 sts plus 4 extra, turn.
Next row (RS): 3 ch (counts as first tr), 2 tr into dc at base of 3 ch, miss 2 dc, 1 dc into next dc, *miss 1 dc, 5 tr into next dc, miss 2 dc, 1 dc into next dc, rep from * to marker.
Fasten off.
Fold shoulder panel along shoulder line so that trim overlaps front cast-off edge and sew together at armhole edge.
See information page for finishing instructions, setting in sleeves using the shallow set-in method. Attach buttons to right front shoulder edge, using "holes" of shoulder panel trim as buttonholes.

Lower crochet trim

With RS facing, using 3.50mm (US E4) crochet hook and yarn D, attach yarn to right side seam level with first rep of chart row 25. Now, working into sts of row 25, cont as folls:
Round 1: work 1 round of ss evenly around entire front and back, ensuring number of ss worked is divisible by 4.
Round 2: 1 ch (does NOT count as st), 1 dc into first ss, *miss 1 ss, 5 tr into next ss, miss 1 ss, 1 dc into next ss, rep from * to end, replacing dc at end of last rep with ss to first dc.
Fasten off.
Work around row 25 of sleeves in same way.

Upper crochet trim

With RS facing, using 3.50mm (US E4) crochet hook and yarn B, attach yarn to right side seam level with first rep of chart row 39. Now, working into sts of row 39, work rounds 1 and 2 as given for lower crochet trim.
Fasten off.

9-12 and 12-18 months, and 2, 3 and 4 years sizes

Work around row 39 of sleeves in same way.

Embroidery

Using yarn B, work a line of bullion knots around first rep of chart row 16 on back, front and sleeves.
Using yarn A, work a line of bullion knots around first rep of chart row 46 on back, front and sleeves (if appropriate).

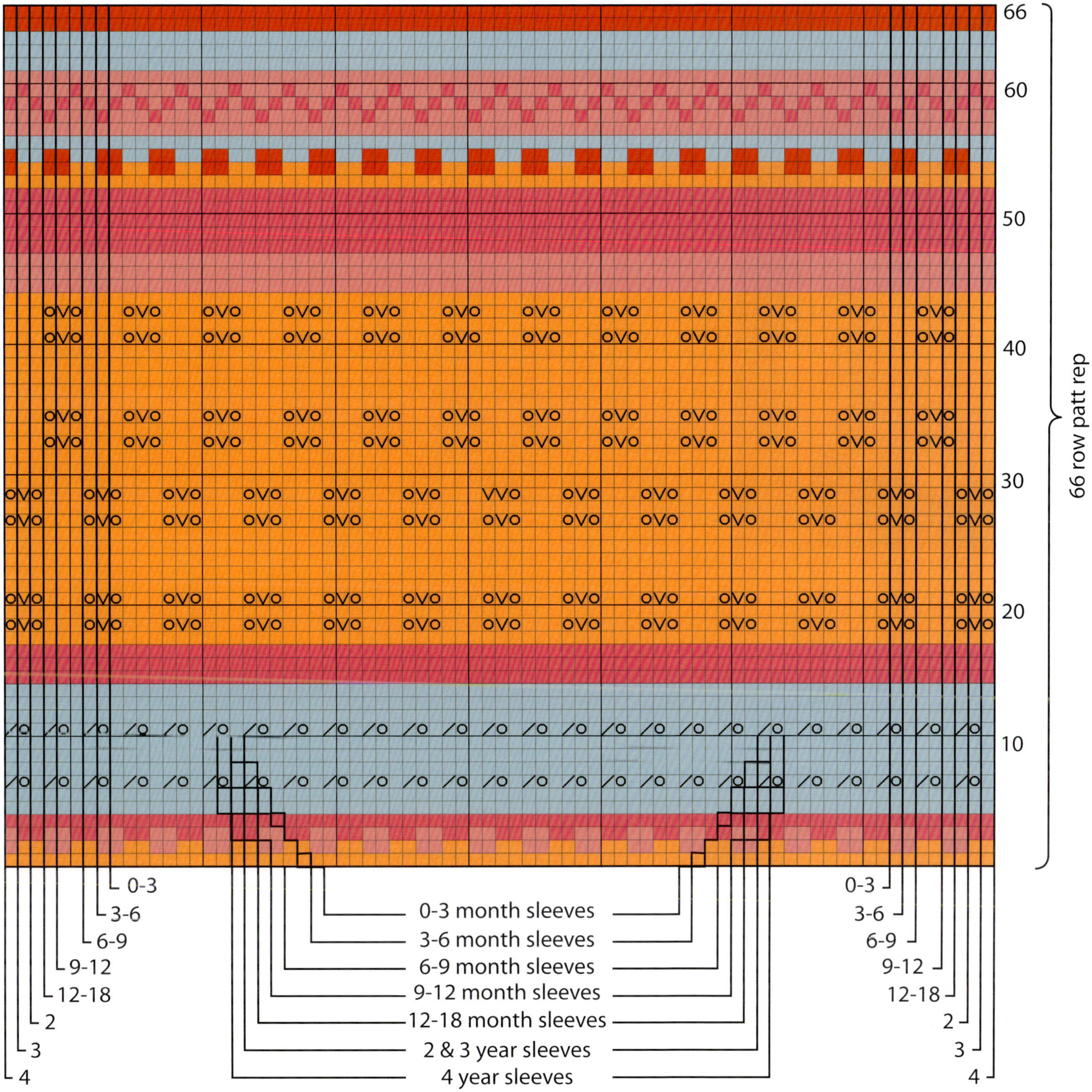

key

A

B

C

D

E

K on RS, P on WS

yfwd

K2tog

S1, K2tog, psso

bob jumper by Marie Wallin

YARN

To fit age	0-3	3-6	6-9	9-12	12-18	months	2	3	4	years
Rowan Fine Milk Cotton	3	3	4	4	4		5	5	5	x 50gm

(photographed in Barley Sugar 081)

NEEDLES

1 pair 2mm (no 14) (US 0) needles, 1 pair 2¾mm (no 12) (US 2) needles & Cable needle

BUTTONS – 2 x 00320

TENSION

30 sts and 38 rows to 10 cm measured over rev st st using 2¾mm (US 2) needles.

SPECIAL ABBREVIATIONS

C4B = slip next 2 sts onto cable needle and leave at back of work, K2, then K2 from cable needle; **C4F** = slip next 2 sts onto cable needle and leave at front of work, K2, then K2 from cable needle; **C6B** = slip next 3 sts onto cable needle and leave at back of work, K3, then K3 from cable needle; **C6F** = slip next 3 sts onto cable needle and leave at front of work, K3, then K3 from cable needle.

BACK

Using 2mm (US 0) needles cast on 79 [81: 85: 87: 91: 93: 97: 99] sts.
Row 1 (RS): K0 [0: 2: 0: 0: 0: 2: 0], P2 [3: 3: 0: 2: 3: 3: 0], *K3, P3, rep from * to last 5 [0: 2: 3: 5: 0: 2: 3] sts, K3 [0: 2: 3: 3: 0: 2: 3], P2 [0: 0: 0: 2: 0: 0: 0].
Row 2: P0 [0: 2: 0: 0: 0: 2: 0], K2 [3: 3: 0: 2: 3: 3: 0], *P3, K3, rep from * to last 5 [0: 2: 3: 5: 0: 2: 3] sts, P3 [0: 2: 3: 3: 0: 2: 3], K2 [0: 0: 0: 2: 0: 0: 0].
These 2 rows form rib.
Work in rib for a further 5 rows, ending with WS facing for next row.
Row 8 (WS): Rib 17 [18: 20: 21: 23: 24: 26: 27], inc in next st, rib 4, inc once in each of next 2 sts, rib 4, inc in next st, rib 2, inc in next st, rib 4, inc once in each of next 7 sts, rib 4, inc in next st, rib 2, inc in next st, rib 4, inc once in each of next 2 sts, rib 4, inc in next st, rib to end. 96 [98: 102: 104: 108: 110: 114: 116] sts.
Change to 2¾mm (US 2) needles.
Beg and ending rows as indicated and repeating the 36 row patt rep throughout, work in patt from chart for body as folls:
Cont straight until back meas 16 [18: 18: 20: 21: 22: 22: 24] cm, ending with RS facing for next row.

Shape armholes

Keeping patt correct, cast off 2 [2: 2: 2: 3: 3: 3: 3] sts at beg of next 2 rows. 92 [94: 98: 100: 102: 104: 108: 110] sts.
Dec 1 st at each end of next 1 [1: 3: 3: 3: 3: 3: 5] rows, then on foll 2 [2: 1: 2: 2: 2: 3: 2] alt rows. 86 [88: 90: 90: 92: 94: 96: 96] sts.
Cont straight until armhole meas 9 [9: 10: 10: 11: 11: 12: 12] cm, ending with RS facing for next row.

Shape shoulders and back neck

Cast off 6 [6: 7: 6: 7: 7: 7: 7] sts at beg of next 2 rows. 74 [76: 76: 78: 78: 80: 82: 82] sts.
Next row (RS): Cast off 6 [6: 7: 6: 7: 7: 7: 7] sts, patt until there are 10 [10: 9: 10: 9: 9: 10: 9] sts on right needle and turn, leaving rem sts on a holder.
Work each side of neck separately.
Cast off 3 sts at beg of next row.
Cast off rem 7 [7: 6: 7: 6: 6: 7: 6] sts.
With RS facing, rejoin yarn to rem sts, cast off centre 42 [44: 44: 46: 46: 48: 48: 50] sts, patt to end.
Complete to match first side, reversing shapings.

FRONT

Work as given for back until 16 [18: 18: 18: 20: 20: 20: 22] rows less have been worked than on back to beg of shoulder shaping, ending with RS facing for next row.

Shape neck

Next row (RS): Patt 27 [28: 29: 28: 30: 30: 31: 31] sts and turn, leaving rem sts on a holder.
Work each side of neck separately.
Keeping patt correct, dec 1 st at neck edge of next 8 rows, then on foll 0 [1: 1: 1: 2: 2: 2: 3] alt rows. 19 [19: 20: 19: 20: 20: 21: 20] sts.
Work 1 row, ending with RS facing for next row. (Note: Left front "shoulder edge" is 6 rows below other shoulder edges as buttonhole border is added along this edge.)

Shape shoulder

Cast off 6 [6: 7: 6: 7: 7: 7: 7] sts at beg of next and foll alt row.
Work 1 row.
Cast off rem 7 [7: 6: 7: 6: 6: 7: 6] sts.
With RS facing, rejoin yarn to rem sts, cast off centre 32 [32: 32: 34: 32: 34: 34: 34] sts, patt to end.
Keeping patt correct, dec 1 st at neck edge of next 8 rows, then on foll 0 [1: 1: 1: 2: 2: 2: 3] alt rows. 19 [19: 20: 19: 20: 20: 21: 20] sts.
Work 8 rows, ending with WS facing for next row.

Shape shoulder
Cast off 6 [6: 7: 6: 7: 7: 7: 7] sts at beg of next and foll alt row.
Work 1 row.
Cast off rem 7 [7: 6: 7: 6: 6: 7: 6] sts.

SLEEVES

Using 2mm (US 0) needles cast on 39 [43: 43: 45: 45: 49: 49: 51] sts.
Row 1 (RS): K0 [0: 0: 0: 0: 2: 2: 0], P0 [2: 2: 3: 3: 3: 3: 0], *K3, P3, rep from * to last 3 [5: 5: 0: 0: 2: 2: 3] sts, K3 [3: 3: 0: 0: 2: 2: 3], P0 [2: 2: 0: 0: 0: 0: 0].
Row 2: P0 [0: 0: 0: 0: 2: 2: 0], K0 [2: 2: 3: 3: 3: 3: 0], *P3, K3, rep from * to last 3 [5: 5: 0: 0: 2: 2: 3] sts, P3 [3: 3: 0: 0: 2: 2: 3], K0 [2: 2: 0: 0: 0: 0: 0].
These 2 rows form rib.
Work in rib for a further 5 rows, ending with WS facing for next row.
Row 8 (WS): Rib 8 [10: 10: 11: 11: 13: 13: 14], inc in next st, rib 2, inc in next st, rib 4, inc once in each of next 7 sts, rib 4, inc in next st, rib 2, inc in next st, rib to end. 50 [54: 54: 56: 56: 60: 60: 62] sts.
Change to 2¾mm (US 2) needles.
Beg and ending rows as indicated and repeating the 36 row patt rep throughout, work in patt from chart for sleeve, shaping sides by inc 1 st at each end of next [next: next: 3rd: 3rd: 3rd: 3rd: 3rd] and every foll alt [4th: 4th: 4th: 4th: 4th: 4th: 6th] row to 68 [74: 78: 78: 82: 70: 74: 92] sts, then on every foll 4th [-: -: 6th: 6th: 6th: 6th: -] row until there are 72 [-: -: 80: 84: 86: 90: -] sts, taking inc sts into rev st st.
Cont straight until sleeve meas 12 [15: 17: 19: 21: 24: 26: 29] cm, ending with RS facing for next row.
Shape top
Keeping patt correct, cast off 8 [8: 6: 6: 5: 5: 5: 5] sts at beg of next 6 [4: 4: 2: 4: 2: 12: 10] rows, then - [9: 7: 7: 6: 6: -: 6] sts at beg of foll - [2: 4: 6: 6: 8: -: 2] rows.
Cast off rem 24 [24: 26: 26: 28: 28: 30: 30] sts.

MAKING UP

Press as described on the information page.
Join right shoulder seam using back stitch, or mattress stitch if preferred.
Left back shoulder button border
With RS facing and using 2mm (US 0) needles, pick up and knit 17 sts evenly along left back shoulder edge.
Row 1 (WS): K1, (P3, K3) twice, P3, K1.
Row 2: K4, P3, K3, P3, K4.
These 2 rows form rib.
Work in rib for a further 3 rows, ending with RS facing for next row.
Cast off in rib.
Left front shoulder buttonhole border
With RS facing and using 2mm (US 0) needles, pick up and knit 17 sts evenly along left front shoulder edge.
Work in rib as given for left back shoulder button border for 1 row, ending with RS facing for next row.
Row 2 (RS): K4, P3, K1, yfwd, K2tog (to make a buttonhole), P3, K4.
Work in rib for a further 3 rows, ending with RS facing for next row.
Cast off in rib.
Lay front buttonhole border over back button border so that cast-off edges match pick-up rows and sew together at armhole edge.
Neckband
With RS facing and using 2mm (US 0) needles, beg and ending at top of shoulder borders, pick up and knit 15 [17: 17: 18: 19: 20: 20: 22] sts down left side of neck, 23 [23: 23: 25: 23: 25: 25: 25] sts from front, 15 [17: 17: 18: 19: 20: 20: 22] sts up right side of neck, 37 [39: 39: 41: 41: 43: 43: 45] sts from back, then 5 sts from row-end edge of back button border. 95 [101: 101: 107: 107: 113: 113: 119] sts.
Row 1 (WS): K1, *P3, K3, rep from * to last 4 sts, P3, K1.
Row 2: K2, K2tog, yfrn (to make 2nd buttonhole), *P3, K3, rep from * to last st, K1.
These 2 rows set position of rib.
Work in rib for a further 3 rows, ending with RS facing for next row.
Cast off in rib.
See information page for finishing instructions, setting in sleeves using the shallow set-in method.

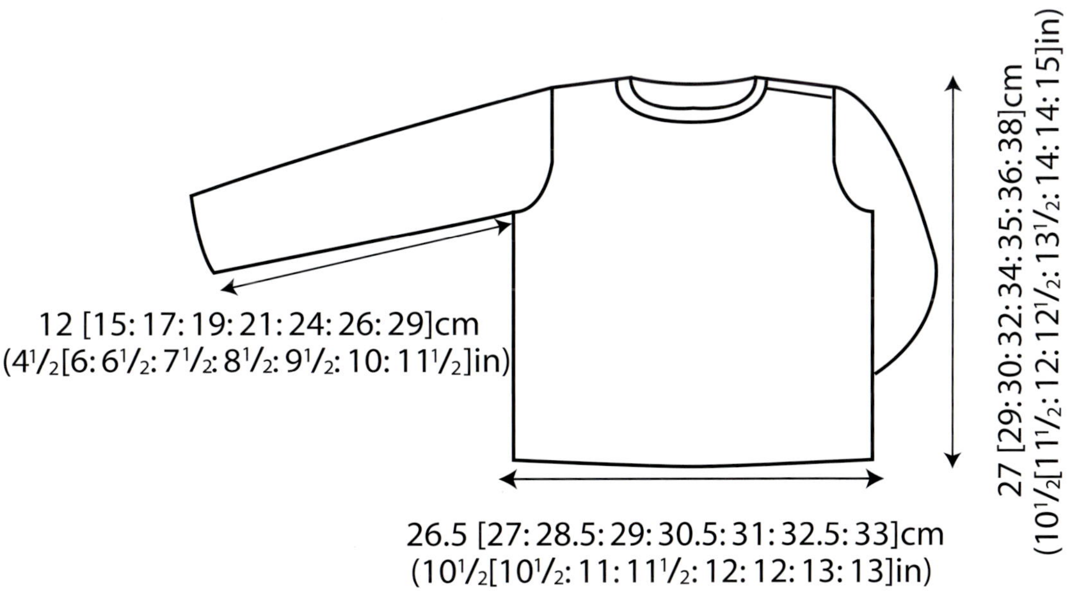

body chart

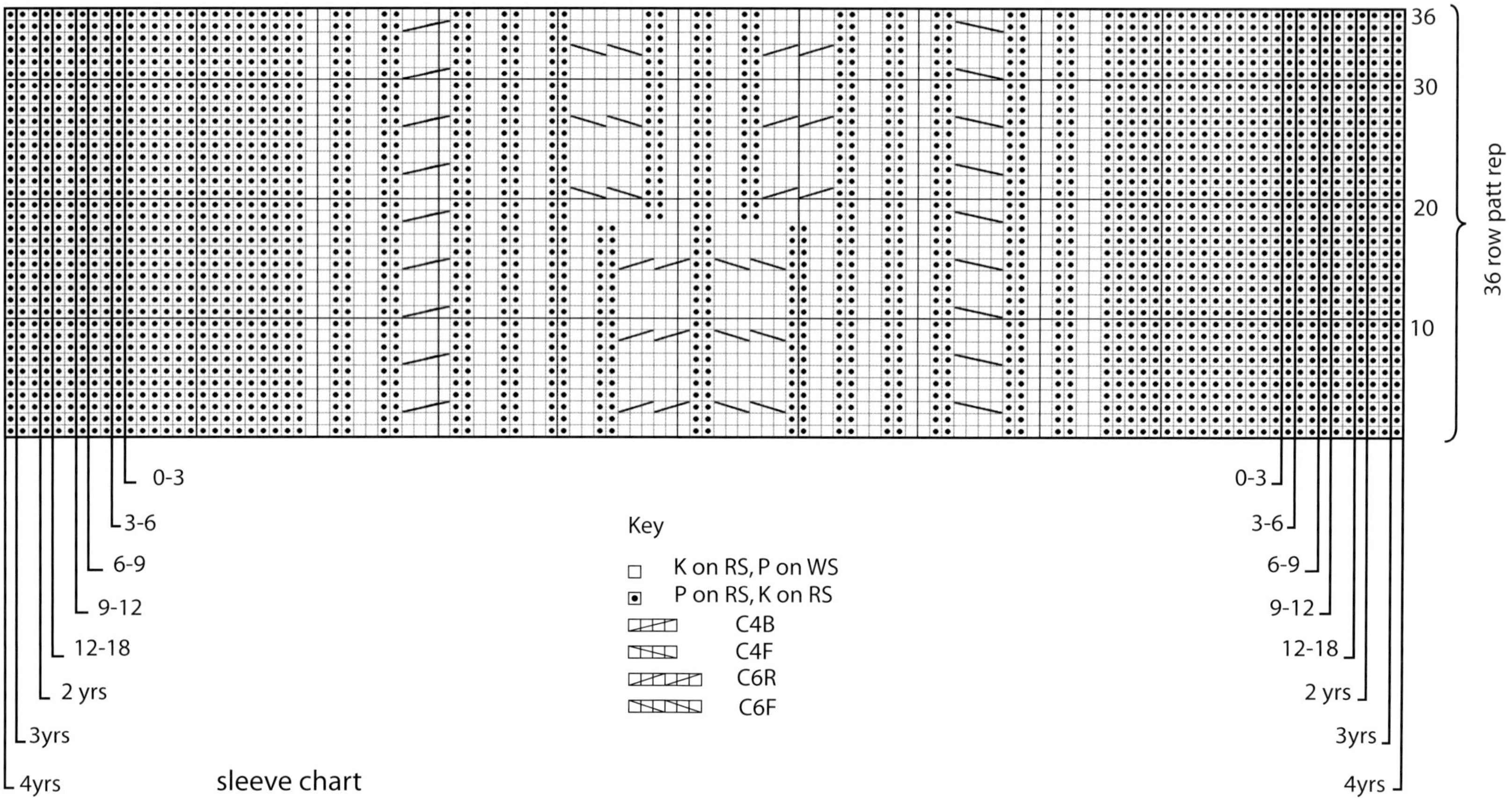

sleeve chart

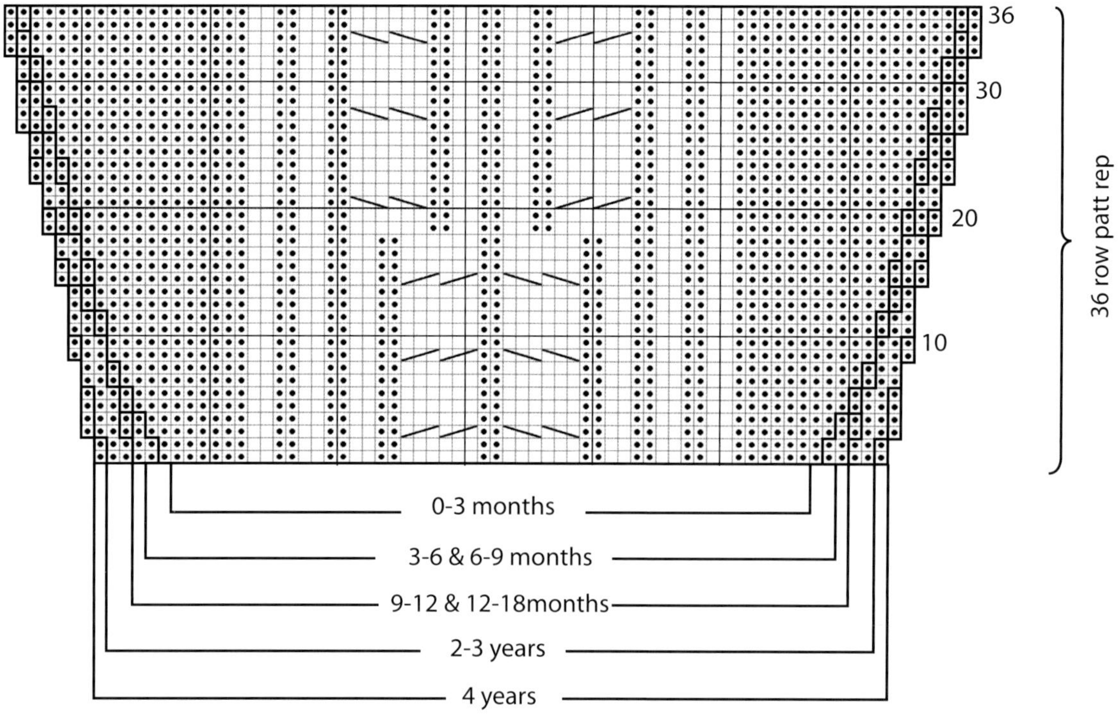

waldo the wonder cat

by Lisa Richardson

YARN

Rowan Fine Milk Cotton

A	Barley Sugar 481	1	x	50gm
B	Dip Dab 485	1	x	50gm
C	Sherbert 480	1	x	50gm
D	Shrimps 483	1	x	50gm
E	Humbugs 484	1	x	50gm
F	Apple Pips 482	1	x	50gm
G	Bon Bon 492	1	x	50gm

NEEDLES

1 pair 2¼mm (no 13) (US 1) needles

EXTRAS - washable toy filling

TENSION

36 sts and 48 rows to 10 cm measured over st st using 2¼mm (US 1) needles.

FINISHED SIZE

Completed toy is approx 18 cm (7 ins) tall.

BACK and FRONT (both alike)

First leg

Using 2¼mm (US 1) needles and yarn A cast on 5 sts.
Beg with a K row, work in st st throughout as folls:
Work 1 row, ending with WS facing for next row.
Inc 1 st at each end of next 2 rows. 9 sts.
Work 7 rows, ending with RS facing for next row.
Break off yarn A and join in yarn E.
Work 21 rows, ending with WS facing for next row.**
Inc 1 st at end of next row. 10 sts.
Break yarn and leave sts on a holder.

Second leg

Work as given for first leg to **.
Inc 1 st at beg of next row. 10 sts.

Join legs

Row 33 (RS): K 10 sts of second leg, turn and cast on 2 sts, turn and K 10 sts of first leg. 22 sts.
Work 3 rows, ending with RS facing for next row.
***Joining in and breaking off colours as required, now work in striped st st as folls:
Rows 37 and 38: Using yarn B.
Rows 39 and 40: Using yarn C.
Rows 41 and 42: Using yarn D.
Rows 43 and 44: Using yarn E.
Rows 45 and 46: Using yarn B.
Rows 47 and 48: Using yarn F.
Rows 49 and 50: Using yarn E.***
Rows 51 and 52: Using yarn G.
Rows 53 and 54: Using yarn D.
Rows 55 and 56: Using yarn C.
Rows 57 and 58: Using yarn F.
Rows 59 and 60: Using yarn B.
Rows 61 and 62: Using yarn C and dec 1 st at each end of both rows. 18 sts.
Break off contrasts and cont in st st using yarn A only.
Dec 1 st at each end of next 2 rows. 14 sts.
Work 2 rows.

Shape head

Inc 1 st at each end of next 3 rows, ending with WS facing for next row. 20 sts.
Work 14 rows.
Inc 1 st at each end of next 2 rows. 24 sts.
Work 1 row, ending with RS facing for next row.
Cast off.

ARMS (both alike)

Using 2¼mm (US 1) needles and yarn A cast on 4 sts.
Beg with a K row, work in st st throughout as folls:
Row 1 (RS): Inc once in each st to end. 8 sts.
Work 7 rows, ending with RS facing for next row.
Now work from *** to *** as given for back and front.
Rows 23 and 24: Using yarn G and dec 1 st at each end of first of these rows. 6 sts.
Rows 25 and 26: Using yarn D and dec 1 st at each end of first of these rows. 4 sts.
Rows 27 and 28: Using yarn C and dec 1 st at each end of first of these rows. 2 sts.
Row 29: Using yarn C, K2tog and fasten off.

MAKING UP

Press as described on the information page.
Join back to front along entire outer edges, leaving an opening to insert toy filling. Insert toy filling and sew opening closed. Join cast-on and row-end edges of each arm to first dec. Insert toy filling. Using photograph as a guide. Sew arms to body. Using yarn A, make a 6 cm long plait and knot one end, leaving a tiny tassel. Attach plait to back to form tail. Using yarn B and photograph as a guide, embroider face onto front.

jake hoodie by Martin Storey

YARN

To fit age	0-3	3-6	6-9	9-12	12-18 months	2	3	4 years	
Rowan Milk Cotton DK									
A Aniseed 090	2	2	2	3	3	3	4	4	x 50gm
B Barley Sugar 081	2	2	2	2	3	3	3	3	x 50gm

NEEDLES

1 pair 3¼mm (no 10) (US 3) needles
1 pair 3¼mm (no 9) (US 5) needles
3¼mm (no 10) (US 3) circular needle

BUTTONS – 5 x 00324

TENSION

22 sts and 30 rows to 10 cm measured over st st using 3¾mm (US 5) needles.

BACK

Using 3¼mm (US 3) needles and yarn A cast on 58 [58: 62: 62: 66: 70: 70: 74] sts.

Row 1 (RS): K2, *P2, K2, rep from * to end.

Row 2: P2, *K2, P2, rep from * to end.

These 2 rows form rib.

Work in rib for a further 6 rows, dec [inc: dec: inc: inc: dec: inc: dec] 1 st at end of last row and ending with RS facing for next row. 57 [59: 61: 63: 67: 69: 71: 73] sts.

Change to 3¾mm (US 5) needles.

Join in yarn B.

Beg with a K row, work in striped st st as folls:

Using yarn B, work 8 rows.

Using yarn A, work 8 rows.

These 16 rows form striped st st.

Work in striped st st until back meas 16 [18: 18: 20: 20: 22: 22: 24] cm, ending with RS facing for next row.

Shape armholes

Keeping stripes correct, cast off 2 [2: 2: 2: 3: 3: 3: 3] sts at beg of next 2 rows. 53 [55: 57: 59: 61: 63: 65: 67] sts.

Dec 1 st at each end of next 1 [1: 1: 1: 1: 1: 3: 3] rows, then on foll 0 [1: 1: 2: 2: 2: 1: 1] alt rows. 51 [51: 53: 53: 55: 57: 57: 59] sts.

Cont straight until armhole meas 10 [10: 11: 11: 12: 12: 13: 13] cm, ending with RS facing for next row.

Shape shoulders and back neck

Next row (RS): Cast off 5 [5: 5: 5: 6: 6: 6: 6] sts, K until there are 9 [8: 9: 9: 9: 9: 9: 9] sts on right needle and turn, leaving rem sts on a holder.

Work each side of neck separately.

Cast off 3 sts at beg of next row.

Cast off rem 6 [5: 6: 6: 6: 6: 6: 6] sts.

With RS facing, rejoin appropriate yarn to rem sts, cast off centre 23 [25: 25: 25: 25: 27: 27: 29] sts, K to end.

Complete to match first side, reversing shapings.

LEFT FRONT

Using 3¼mm (US 3) needles and yarn A cast on 27 [27: 27: 31: 31: 35: 35: 35] sts.

Row 1 (RS): K2, *P2, K2, rep from * to last st, K1.

Row 2: K1, P2, *K2, P2, rep from * to end.

These 2 rows form rib.

Work in rib for a further 6 rows, - [inc: inc: dec: inc: dec: dec: -] - [1: 2: 1: 1: 2: 1: -] sts evenly across last row and ending with RS facing for next row. 27 [28: 29: 30: 32: 33: 34: 35] sts.

Change to 3¾mm (US 5) needles.

Join in yarn B.

Beg with a K row and 8 rows using yarn B, work in striped st st as given for back until left front matches back to beg of armhole shaping, ending with RS facing for next row.

Shape armhole

Keeping stripes correct, cast off 2 [2: 2: 2: 3: 3: 3: 3] sts at beg of next row. 25 [26: 27: 28: 29: 30: 31: 32] sts.

Work 1 row.

Dec 1 st at armhole edge of next 1 [1: 1: 1: 1: 1: 3: 3] rows, then on foll 0 [1: 1: 2: 2: 2: 1: 1] alt rows. 24 [24: 25: 25: 26: 27: 27: 28] sts.

Cont straight until left front matches back to beg of shoulder shaping, ending with RS facing for next row.

Shape shoulders

Cast off 5 [5: 5: 5: 6: 6: 6: 6] sts at beg of next row, then 6 [5: 6: 6: 6: 6: 6: 6] sts at beg of foll alt row.

Work 1 row, ending with RS facing for next row.

Leave rem 13 [14: 14: 14: 14: 15: 15: 16] sts on a holder.

RIGHT FRONT

Using 3¼mm (US 3) needles and yarn A cast on 27 [27: 27: 31: 31: 35: 35: 35] sts.

Row 1 (RS): K3, *P2, K2, rep from * to end.

Row 2: P2, *K2, P2, rep from * to last st, K1.

These 2 rows form rib.

Complete to match left front, reversing shapings, ensuring right front ends with RS facing for next row.

Do NOT break yarn but set aside this ball of yarn for hood.

SLEEVES

Using 3¼mm (US 3) needles and yarn A cast on 30 [30: 30: 34: 34: 34: 34: 38] sts.

Work in rib as given for back for 8 rows, dec [inc: inc: dec: dec: inc: inc: dec] 1 st at centre of last row and ending with RS facing for next row. 29 [31: 31: 33: 33: 35: 35: 37] sts.

Change to 3¾mm (US 5) needles.

Join in yarn B.

Beg with a K row, work in striped st st as folls:

Using yarn B, work 4 rows, inc 1 st at each end of next [next: next: 3rd: 3rd: 3rd: 3rd: -] and foll alt [alt: alt: -: -: -: -: -] row. 33 [35: 35: 35: 35: 37: 37: 37] sts.

Using yarn A, work 4 rows, inc 1 st at each end of first [first: first: 3rd: 3rd: 3rd: 3rd: first] and foll alt [alt: -: -: -: -: -: -] of these rows. 37 [39: 37: 37: 37: 39: 39: 39] sts.

These 8 rows form striped st st and beg sleeve shaping.

Work in striped st st, shaping sides by inc 1 st at each end of next [3rd: next: 3rd: 3rd: 3rd: 3rd: 3rd] and every foll alt [4th: 4th: 4th: 4th: 4th: 4th: 6th] row to 49 [49: 51: 49: 55: 43: 45: 53] sts, then on every foll - [-: -: 6th: -: 6th: 6th: 8th] row until there are - [-: -: 51: -: 55: 57: 57] sts.

Cont straight until sleeve meas 12 [15: 17: 19: 21: 24: 26: 29] cm, ending with RS facing for next row.

Shape top

Keeping stripes correct, cast off 4 sts at beg of next 8 [8: 8: 8: 10: 10: 10: 10] rows.

Cast off rem 17 [17: 19: 19: 15: 15: 17: 17] sts.

MAKING UP

Press as described on the information page.

Join both shoulder seams using back stitch, or mattress stitch if preferred.

Hood

With RS facing, using 3¾mm (US 5) needles and ball of yarn set aside with right front (or correct yarn to keep stripes on fronts correct), K 13 [14: 14: 14: 14: 15: 15: 16] sts on right front holder, pick up and knit 29 [31: 31: 31: 31: 33: 33: 35] sts from back, then K 13 [14: 14: 14: 14: 15: 15: 16] sts on left front holder. 55 [59: 59: 59: 59: 63: 63: 67] sts.

Keeping stripes correct throughout hood as set by fronts, cont as folls:

Row 1 (WS): P8 [12: 10: 8: 6: 10: 8: 12], inc next st, (P1, inc in next st) 19 [17: 19: 21: 23: 21: 23: 21] times, P to end. 75 [77: 79: 81: 83: 85: 87: 89] sts.

Cont in striped st st until hood meas approx 18 [19: 20: 21: 22: 23: 24: 25] cm from pick-up row, ending after 8th row of a stripe and with RS facing for next row.

Shape back

Place marker on centre st of last row.

Next row (RS): K to within 2 sts of marked st, K2tog, K marked st, K2tog tbl, K to end.

Next row: Purl.

Rep last 2 rows twice more. 69 [71: 73: 75: 77: 79: 81: 83] sts.

Next row (RS): K to within 2 sts of marked st, K2tog, K marked st, K2tog tbl, K to end.

Next row: P to within 2 sts of marked st, P2tog tbl, P marked st, P2tog, P to end.

Rep last 2 rows twice more. 57 [59: 61: 63: 65: 67: 69: 71] sts.

Next row (RS): K27 [28: 29: 30: 31: 32: 33: 34], K2tog and turn.

Using a spare needle, fold hood in half with RS together, and join top seam by casting off both sets of 28 [29: 30: 31: 32: 33: 34: 35] sts together.

Front and hood border

With RS facing, using 3¼mm (US 3) circular needle and yarn A, beg and ending at cast-on edges, pick up and knit 65 [70: 72: 77: 79: 84: 87: 91] sts up right front opening edge to hood pick-up row, 50 [53: 55: 58: 60: 61: 64: 66] sts up right side of hood to top seam, 50 [53: 55: 58: 60: 61: 64: 66] sts down left side of hood to hood pick-up row, then 65 [70: 72: 77: 79: 84: 87: 91] sts down left front opening edge. 230 [246: 254: 270: 278: 290: 302: 314] sts.

Beg with row 2, work in rib as given for back for 3 rows, ending with RS facing for next row.

For a girl

Row 4 (RS): Rib 2, *work 2 tog, yrn (to make a buttonhole), rib 10 [11: 11: 12: 13: 14: 15: 16], rep from * 3 times more, work 2 tog, yrn (to make 5th buttonhole), rib to end.

For a boy

Row 4 (RS): Rib to last 53 [57: 57: 61: 65: 69: 73: 77], *work 2 tog, yrn (to make a buttonhole), rib 10 [11: 11: 12: 13: 14: 15: 16], rep from * 3 times more, work 2 tog, yrn (to make 5th buttonhole), rib 3.

For a girl or a boy

Work in rib for a further 3 rows, ending with RS facing for next row.

Cast off in rib.

See information page for finishing instructions, setting in sleeves using the shallow set-in method.

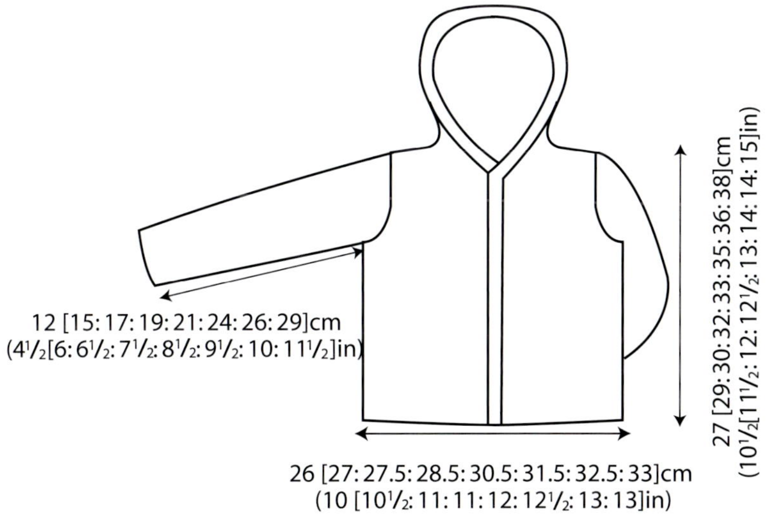

lucy shoes by Lisa Richardson

YARN

To fit age

	0-3	3-6	6-9	9-12	12-18	months
Rowan Milk Cotton DK						
	1	1	1	1	1	x 50gm

(photographed in either Dip Dab 085, Barley Sugar 081, Tutti Fruitti 087, Sherbert 080)

NEEDLES

1 pair 3¾mm (no 9) (US 5) needles

EXTRAS – Approx 40 cm of lace trim for lace trimmed shoes. Approx 2.50 m of 6 mm wide satin ribbon for shoes with ankle ribbons. 2 buttons for shoes with straps. Approx 40 cm of 1 cm wide organza ribbon for shoes with straps and bows. Approx 1 m of 3 mm wide satin ribbon for shoes with straps and flower embroidery.

TENSION

22 sts and 41 rows to 10 cm measured over moss st using 3¾mm (US 5) needles.

Shoes without straps

LEFT SHOE

Using 3¾mm (US 5) needles cast on 14 [15: 19: 20: 24] sts.
Row 1 (RS): K0 [1: 1: 0: 0], *P1, K1, rep from * to end.
Row 2: Inc in first st, *P1, K1, rep from * to last 1 [2: 2: 1: 1] sts, P0 [1: 1: 0: 0], inc in last st. 16 [17: 21: 22: 26] sts.
These 2 rows form moss st and beg shaping.
Keeping moss st correct throughout, cont as folls:
Inc 1 st at each end of 2nd [next: 2nd: next: 2nd] and 0 [1: 1: 2: 2] foll alt rows. 18 [21: 25: 28: 32] sts.
Work 3 rows.
Dec 1 st at each end of next and foll 1 [1: 2: 2: 3] alt rows, then on foll 0 [1: 0: 1: 0] row, ending with RS facing for next row.
14 [15: 19: 20: 24] sts.
This completes sole section.
Shape upper
Next row (RS): Moss st to end, turn and cast on 4 [5: 6: 7: 8] sts (for heel section). 18 [20: 25: 27: 32] sts.
Work 1 row.
Inc 1 st at toe edge of next 1 [2: 1: 2: 1] rows, then on foll 3 [3: 4: 4: 5] alt rows, ending with WS [RS: WS: RS: WS] facing for next row. 22 [25: 30: 33: 38] sts.**
Shape opening for foot
0-3, 6-9 and 12-18 months sizes
Cast off 12 [-: 16: -: 20] sts at beg of next row. 10 [-: 14: -: 18] sts.
Work 4 [-: 8: -: 12] rows, ending with RS facing for next row.
Next row (RS): Moss st to end, turn and cast on 12 [-: 16: -: 20] sts (for other side of heel). 22 [-: 30: -: 38] sts.
3-6 and 9-12 month sizes
Next row (RS): Moss st – [12: -: 16: -] sts,
cast off rem – [13: -: 17: -] sts. – [12: -: 16: -] sts.
Rejoin yarn with WS facing and cont as folls:
Work – [6: -: 10: -] rows, ending with WS facing for next row.
Cast on – [13: -: 17: -] sts at beg of next row (for other side of heel). – [25: -: 33: -] sts.
All sizes
***Work 1 row.
Dec 1 st at toe edge of next and foll 3 [3: 4: 4: 5] alt rows, then on foll 0 [1: 0: 1: 0] row, ending with WS facing for next row.
Cast off rem 18 [20: 25: 27: 32] sts.

RIGHT SHOE

Work exactly as given for left shoe, but reading RS for WS and vice versa (to reverse all shaping).

MAKING UP

Press as described on the information page.
Join straight row-end edges of heel sections to form heel seam using back stitch, or mattress stitch if preferred.
Easing in fullness of upper to fit sole, sew upper to sole.
For lace trimmed shoes, sew lace trim to foot opening edge.
For shoes with ankle ribbons, cut ribbon into 4 equal lengths.
Using photograph as a guide, sew one end of each piece to inside of foot opening edge at front "corners". Cross ribbons, then thread ends through sides of foot opening.

Shoes with straps

LEFT SHOE

Work as given for left shoe without strap to **.
Shape opening for foot
0-3, 6-9 and 12-18 months sizes
Next row (WS): Cast off 6 [-: 8: -: 12] sts, moss st until there are

3 [-: 4: -: 4] sts on right needle after cast-off and slip these sts onto a holder for strap, cast off next 3 [-: 4: -: 4] sts, moss st to end. 10 [-: 14: -: 18] sts.
Work 4 [-: 8: -: 12] rows, ending with RS facing for next row.
Next row (RS): Moss st to end, turn and cast on 12 [-: 16: -: 20] sts (for other side of heel). 22 [-: 30: -: 38] sts.
3-6 and 9-12 month sizes
Next row (RS): Moss st — [12: -: 16: -] sts, cast off next — [3: -: 4: -] sts, moss st until there are — [3: -: 4: -] sts on right needle after cast-off and slip these sts onto a holder for strap, cast off rem — [7: -: 9: -] sts. — [12: -: 16: -] sts.
Rejoin yarn with WS facing and cont as folls:
Work — [6: -: 10: -] rows, ending with WS facing for next row.
Cast on — [13: -: 17: -] sts at beg of next row (for other side of heel). — [25: -: 33: -] sts.
All sizes
Complete as given for left shoe without strap from ***.

RIGHT SHOE

Work exactly as given for left shoe, but reading RS for WS and vice versa (to reverse all shaping).

MAKING UP

Press as described on the information page.
Straps (both alike)
Rejoin yarn to 3 [3: 4: 4: 4] sts left on strap holder with RS [WS: RS: WS: RS] facing and moss st across these sts.
Cont in moss st for a further 5 [7: 9: 11: 13] rows.
Next row (buttonhole row): Moss st 1 [1: 2: 2: 2] sts, yrn (to make a buttonhole), work 2 tog.
Work 2 rows.
Next row: (Work 2 tog) 1 [1: 2: 2: 2] times, moss st 1 [1: 0: 0: 0] st. 2 sts.
Next row: Work 2 tog and fasten off.
Join straight row-end edges of heel sections to form heel seam using back stitch, or mattress stitch if preferred. Easing in fullness of upper to fit sole, sew upper to sole. Attach button to side of shoe to correspond with buttonhole in strap.
For shoes with bows, cut ribbon into 2 equal lengths. Tie each length in a bow, then attach bow to strap as in photograph.
For shoes with flower embroidery, embroider flower onto top of foot by working 5 lazy daisy stitches radiating out from one point using the ribbon.

marcus slipover by Martin Storey

YARN

To fit age

	0-3	3-6	6-9	9-12	12-18	months	2	3	4		years
Rowan Milk Cotton DK											
A Bonfire Toffee 091											
	2	2	2	2	3		3	3	3	x	50gm
B Aniseed 090											
	1	1	1	1	1		1	1	1	x	50gm
C Tutti Fruitti 087											
	1	1	1	1	1		1	1	1	x	50gm
D Barley Sugar 081											
	1	1	1	1	1		1	1	1	x	50gm

NEEDLES

1 pair 3¼mm (no 10) (US 3) needles
1 pair 3¾mm (no 9) (US 5) needles
3¼mm (no 10) (US 3) circular needle

TENSION

22 sts and 38 rows to 10 cm measured over moss st using 3¾mm (US 5) needles.

BACK

Using 3¼mm (US 3) needles and yarn B cast on 54 [58: 58: 62: 62: 66: 70: 70] sts.
Row 1 (RS): K2, *P2, K2, rep from * to end.
Break off yarn B and join in yarn C.
Row 2: P2, *K2, P2, rep from * to end.
These 2 rows form rib.
Using yarn C, work 1 row more in rib.
Break off yarn C and join in yarn D.
Using yarn D, work a further 3 rows in rib, inc [dec: inc: dec: inc: inc: dec: inc] 1 st at end of last row and ending with RS facing for next row. 55 [57: 59: 61: 63: 67: 69: 71] sts.
Break off yarn D and join in yarn A.
Change to 3¾mm (US 5) needles.
Next row (RS): Knit.
Now work in moss st as folls:
Row 1 (WS): K1, *P1, K1, rep from * to end.
Row 2: As row 1.
These 2 rows form moss st.
Cont in moss st until back meas 14 [15: 16: 17: 18: 19: 20: 21] cm, ending with RS facing for next row.

Shape armholes

Keeping moss st correct, cast off 3 sts at beg of next 2 rows. 49 [51: 53: 55: 57: 61: 63: 65] sts.
Dec 1 st at each end of next 1 [1: 1: 3: 3: 3: 3: 5] rows, then on foll 1 [2: 2: 1: 1: 3: 3: 2] alt rows. 45 [45: 47: 47: 49: 49: 51: 51] sts.**
Cont straight until armhole meas 10 [10: 11: 11: 12: 12: 13: 13] cm, ending with RS facing for next row.

Shape shoulders and back neck

Next row (RS): Cast off 4 [4: 4: 4: 5: 4: 5: 5] sts, moss st until there are 8 [7: 8: 8: 8: 8: 8: 8] sts on right needle and turn, leaving rem sts on a holder.
Work each side of neck separately.
Cast off 3 sts at beg of next row.
Cast off rem 5 [4: 5: 5: 5: 5: 5: 5] sts.
With RS facing, rejoin yarn to rem sts, cast off centre 21 [23: 23: 23: 23: 25: 25: 25] sts, moss st to end.
Complete to match first side, reversing shapings.

FRONT

Work as given for back to **.
Work 7 [5: 7: 7: 7: 3: 5: 5] rows, ending with RS facing for next row.

Divide for neck

Next row (RS): Moss st 22 [22: 23: 23: 24: 24: 25: 25] sts and turn, leaving rem sts on a holder.
Work each side of neck separately.
Dec 1 st at neck edge of next 8 [10: 8: 8: 4: 6: 4: 4] rows, then on every foll alt row until 9 [8: 9: 9: 10: 9: 10: 10] sts rem.
Cont straight until front matches back to beg of shoulder shaping, ending with RS facing for next row.

Shape shoulder

Cast off 4 [4: 4: 4: 5: 4: 5: 5] sts at beg of next row.
Work 1 row.
Cast off rem 5 [4: 5: 5: 5: 5: 5: 5] sts.
With RS facing, slip centre st onto a holder, rejoin yarn to rem sts, moss st to end.
Complete to match first side, reversing shapings.

MAKING UP

Press as described on the information page.
Join both shoulder seams using back stitch, or mattress stitch if preferred.

Neckband

With RS facing, using 3¼mm (US 3) circular needle and yarn D, pick up and knit 28 [28: 32: 32: 36: 36: 40: 40] sts down left side of neck, K st from holder at base of V and mark this st with a coloured thread, pick up and knit 28 [28: 32: 32: 36: 36: 40: 40] sts up right side of neck, then 30 [30: 30: 30: 30: 34: 34: 34] sts from back. 87 [87: 95: 95: 103: 107: 115: 115] sts.

Round 1 (RS): *K2, P2, rep from * to marked st, K marked st, P2, **K2, P2, rep from ** to end.

This round sets position of rib.

Keeping rib correct, cont as folls:

Round 2: Rib to within 1 st of marked st, slip 2 sts as though to K2tog (marked st is 2nd of these 2 sts), K1, pass 2 slipped sts over, rib to end.

Break off yarn D and join in yarn C.

Rep round 2 twice more.

Break off yarn C and join in yarn B.

Rep round 1 once more.

Cast off loosely in rib still decreasing either side of marked st as before.

Armhole borders (both alike)

With RS facing, using 3¼mm (US 3) needles and yarn D, pick up and knit 54 [54: 58: 58: 62: 62: 68: 68] sts evenly all round armhole edge.

Beg with row 2, work in rib as given for back for 2 rows.

Break off yarn D and join in yarn C.

Work 2 rows more in rib.

Break off yarn C and join in yarn B.

Work 1 row more in rib, ending with RS facing for next row.

Cast off in rib.

See information page for finishing instructions.

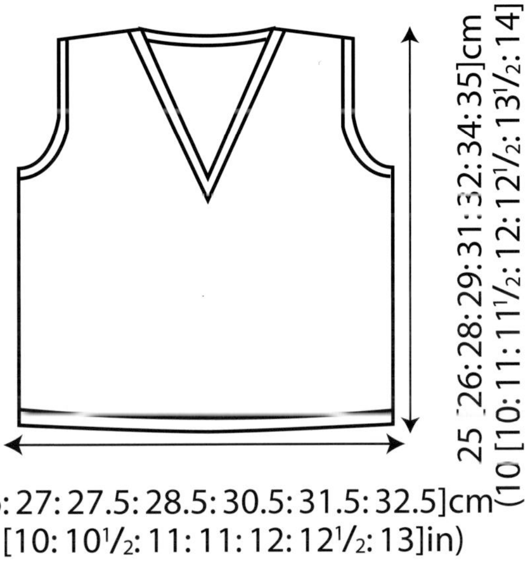

polly cardi by Marie Wallin

YARN

To fit age

	0-3	3-6	6-9	9-12	12-18	months	2	3	4		years
Rowan Milk Cotton DK	3	4	4	4	5		5	5	6	x	50gm

(photographed in Dip Dab 085)

NEEDLES

1 pair 3¾mm (no 9) (US 5) needles
3.50mm (no 9) (US E4) crochet hook

BUTTONS – 4 x 00321

TENSION

22 sts and 40 rows to 10 cm measured over g st using 3¾mm (US 5) needles.

UK CROCHET ABBREVIATIONS

ch = chain; **ss** = slip stitch; **dc** = double crochet; **htr** = half treble; **tr** = treble; **ttr** = triple treble.

BACK

Using 3¾mm (US 5) needles cast on 55 [57: 59: 61: 63: 67: 69: 71] sts.
Work in g st until back meas 9 [11: 11: 12: 13: 14: 15: 16] cm, ending with RS facing for next row.

Shape raglan armholes

Cast off 3 sts at beg of next 2 rows.
49 [51: 53: 55: 57: 61: 63: 65] sts.
Next row (RS): P4, K2tog, K to last 6 sts, K2tog tbl, P4.
Next row: Knit.
Next row: P4, K to last 4 sts, P4.
Next row: Knit.
Next row: P4, K to last 4 sts, P4.
Next row: Knit.
Last 6 rows set the sts and raglan armhole shaping.
Cont as set, dec 1 st at each end of next and 6 [6: 6: 4: 4: 2: 2: 0] foll 6th rows, then on 3 [3: 4: 7: 8: 11: 12: 15] foll 4th rows.
27 [29: 29: 29: 29: 31: 31: 31] sts.
Work 3 rows, ending with RS facing for next row.
Cast off.

LEFT FRONT

Using 3¾mm (US 5) needles cast on 31 [32: 33: 34: 35: 37: 38: 39] sts.
Work in g st until left front matches back to beg of raglan armhole shaping, ending with RS facing for next row.

Shape raglan armholes

Cast off 3 sts at beg of next row. 28 [29: 30: 31: 32: 34: 35: 36] sts.
Work 1 row.
Working all raglan shaping as given for back, dec 1 st at raglan armhole edge of next and 7 [6: 7: 5: 5: 3: 3: 1] foll 6th rows, then on 0 [0: 0: 3: 4: 7: 8: 10] foll 4th rows.
20 [22: 22: 22: 22: 23: 23: 24] sts.
Work 1 [5: 3: 3: 1: 1: 1: 3] rows, ending with RS facing for next row.

Shape neck

Next row (RS): P4, (K2tog) 0 [1: 1: 1: 0: 0: 0: 1] times, K4 [4: 4: 4: 7: 7: 7: 7], cast off last 12 [12: 12: 12: 11: 12: 12: 11] sts.
With WS facing, rejoin yarn to rem 8 [9: 9: 9: 11: 11: 11: 12] sts, K to end.
Keeping raglan shaping correct, dec 1 st at neck edge of next 1 [3: 3: 3: 5: 5: 5: 6] rows and at same time dec 1 st at raglan armhole edge of 0 [0: 0: 0: 2nd: 2nd: 2nd: 4th] row.
7 [6: 6: 6: 5: 5: 5: 5] sts.

0-3 months only

Next row (RS): P4, K3tog. 5 sts.
Next row: K2tog, K3.
Next row: P2, P2tog.
Next row: K2tog, K1. 2 sts.

3-6, 6-9 and 9-12 months only

Next row (RS): P3, P3tog. 4 sts.
Next row: K2tog, K2.
Next row:P1, P2tog. 2 sts.
Next row:K2.

4 years only

Next row (WS): K5.

12-18 months, and 2 and 3 years only

Next row (RS): P2, P3tog. 3 sts.
Next row: K3.
Next row:P1, P2tog. 2 sts.
Next row: K2.

All sizes

Next row (RS): P2tog and fasten off.

Mark positions for 4 buttons along left front opening edge - first to come in row 17, last to come 1.5 cm below neck shaping, and rem 2 buttons evenly spaced between.

RIGHT FRONT

Using 3¾mm (US 5) needles cast on 31 [32: 33: 34: 35: 37: 38: 39] sts.
Work in g st for 16 rows, ending with RS facing for next row.
Row 17 (buttonhole row) (RS): K2, K2tog, yfwd (to make a buttonhole), K to end.
Working a further 3 buttonholes in this way to correspond with positions marked for buttons, complete to match left front, reversing shapings.

SLEEVES

Using 3¾mm (US 5) needles cast on 27 [29: 29: 31: 31: 33: 33: 35] sts.
Work in g st, shaping sides by inc 1 st at each end of 3rd [5th: 5th: 5th: 5th: 7th: 7th: 7th] and every foll 4th [6th: 6th: 6th: 6th: 8th: 8th: 8th] row to 33 [37: 37: 35: 35: 43: 49: 39] sts, then on every foll 6th [8th: 8th: 8th: 8th: 10th: 10th: 10th] row until there are 41 [43: 45: 47: 49: 51: 53: 55] sts.
Cont straight until sleeve meas 12 [15: 17: 19: 21: 24: 26: 29] cm, ending with RS facing for next row.

Shape raglan

Cast off 3 sts at beg of next 2 rows.
35 [37: 39: 41: 43: 45: 47: 49] sts.
Working all raglan shaping as given for back, dec 1 st at each end of next and foll 1 [3: 3: 5: 5: 7: 7: 9] alt rows, then on every foll 4th row until 11 sts rem.
Work 3 rows, ending with RS facing for next row.
Next row (RS): P4, sl 1, K2tog, psso, P4. 9 sts.
Work 3 rows, ending with RS facing for next row.

Left sleeve only

Place marker at beg of last row to denote top of left front raglan edge.
Next row (RS): P4, P2tog, P1, P2tog. 7 sts.
Next row: K2tog, K5.
Next row: P4, P2tog. 5 sts.
Next row:K5.
Next row: P2, P3tog. 3 sts.
Next row:K3.
Next row: P1, P2tog.

Right sleeve only

Place marker at end of last row to denote top of right front raglan edge.
Next row (RS): P2tog, P1, P2tog, P4. 7 sts.
Next row: K5, K2tog.
Next row: P2tog, P4. 5 sts.
Next row: K5.
Next row: P3tog, P2. 3 sts.
Next row: K3.
Next row:P2tog, P1.

Both sleeves

Next row (WS): K2.
Next row: P2tog and fasten off.

MAKING UP

Press as described on the information page.
Join all raglan seams using back stitch, or mattress stitch if preferred. Join side and sleeve seams.

Body edging

With RS facing and using 3.50mm (US E4) crochet hook, attach yarn to base of left side seam, 1 ch (does NOT count as st), spacing sts evenly into knitted edges now work around entire lower, front opening and neck edges as folls: *3 dc into edge, 4 ch, ss to top of dc just worked, rep from * to end, ss to first dc. Fasten off.

Cuff edging

Work as given for body edging, attaching yarn at base of sleeve seam and working evenly around cast-on edge.

Flower

Using 3.50mm (US E4) crochet hook, make 5 ch and join with a ss to form a ring.
Round 1: 1 ch (does NOT count as st), 10 dc into ring, ss to first dc. 10 sts.
Round 2: 1 ch (does NOT count as st), 1 dc into each dc to end, ss to first dc.
Round 3: 2 ch (counts as first htr), 1 htr into dc at base of 2 ch, 2 htr into each dc to end, ss to top of 2 ch at beg of round. 20 sts.
Round 4: Working into front loops only of sts of previous round: *2 ch, 2 tr into each of next 3 htr, 2 ch, 1 ss into next htr, rep from * 4 times more. 5 inner petals.
Round 5: Working into back loops only of sts of round 3: 1 ss into each of first 2 htr, *4 ch, 2 ttr into each of next 3 htr, 4 ch, 1 ss into next htr, rep from * 4 times more. 5 outer petals.
Fasten off.
See information page for finishing instructions. Using photograph as a guide, sew flower onto left front.

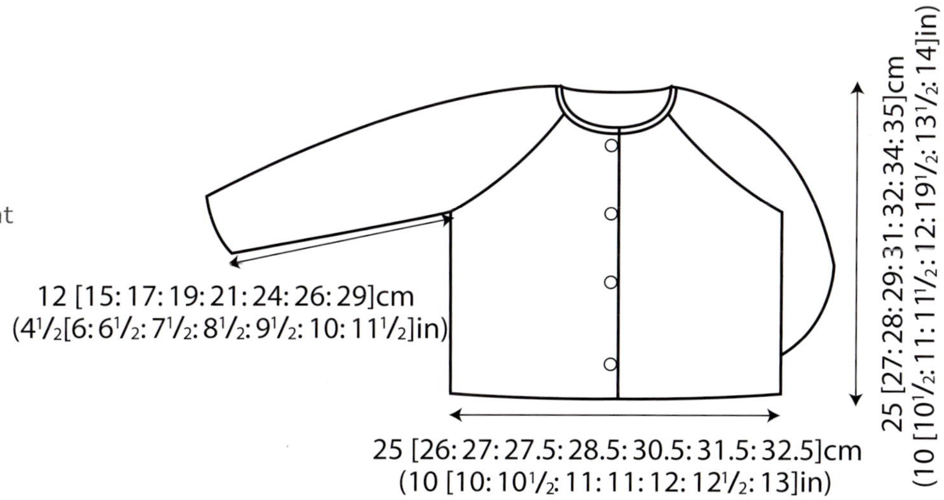

information

Tension

Obtaining the correct tension is perhaps the single factor which can make the difference between a successful garment and a disastrous one. It controls both the shape and size of an article, so any variation, however slight, can distort the finished garment. Different designers feature in our books and it is **their** tension, given at the **start** of each pattern, which you must match. We recommend that you knit a square in pattern and/or stocking stitch (depending on the pattern instructions) of perhaps 5 - 10 more stitches and 5 - 10 more rows than those given in the tension note. Mark out the central 10cm square with pins. If you have too many stitches to 10cm try again using thicker needles, if you have too few stitches to 10cm try again using finer needles. Once you have achieved the correct tension your garment will be knitted to the measurements indicated in the size diagram shown at the end of the pattern.

Sizing & Size Diagram Note

The instructions are given for the smallest size. Where they vary, work the figures in brackets for the larger sizes. **One set of figures refers to all sizes.** Included with most patterns in this magazine is a **'size diagram'**, or sketch of the finished garment and its dimensions. To help you choose the size of garment to knit please refer to the NEW sizing guide on page 102.

Chart Note

Many of the patterns in the book are worked from charts. Each square on a chart represents a stitch and each line of squares a row of knitting. Each colour used is given a different letter and these are shown in the **materials** section, or in the **key** alongside the chart of each pattern. When working from the charts, read odd rows (K) from right to left and even rows (P) from left to right, unless otherwise stated. When working lace from a chart it is important to note that all but the largest size may have to alter the first and last few stitches in order not to lose or gain stitches over the row.

Working a Lace Pattern

When working a lace pattern it is important to remember that if you are unable to work both the increase and corresponding decrease and vica versa, the stitches should be worked in stocking stitch.

Knitting With Colour

There are two main methods of working colour into a knitted fabric: **Intarsia** and **Fairisle** techniques. The first method produces a single thickness of fabric and is usually used where a colour is only required in a particular area of a row and does not form a repeating pattern across the row, as in the fairisle technique.

Intarsia: The simplest way to do this is to cut short lengths of yarn for each motif or block of colour used in a row. Then joining in the various colours at the appropriate point on the row, link one colour to the next by twisting them around each other where they meet on the wrong side to avoid gaps. All ends can then either be darned along the colour join lines, as each motif is completed or then can be " knitted-in" to the fabric of the knitting as each colour is worked into the pattern. This is done in much the same way as"weaving- in" yarns when working the Fairisle technique and does save time darning-in ends. It is essential that the tension is noted for **Intarsia** as this may vary from the stocking stitch if both are used in the same pattern.

Fair isle type knitting: When two or three colours are worked repeatedly across a row, strand the yarn **not** in use loosely behind the stitches being worked. If you are working with more than two colours, treat the "floating" yarns as if they were one yarn and always spread the stitches to their correct width to keep them elastic. It is advisable not to carry the stranded or "floating" yarns over more than three stitches at a time, but to weave them under and over the colour you are working.

The "floating" yarns are therefore caught at the back of the work.

Finishing Instructions

After working for hours knitting a garment, it seems a great pity that many garments are spoiled because such little care is taken in the pressing and finishing process. Follow the following tips for a truly professional-looking garment.

Pressing

Block out each piece of knitting and following the instructions on the ball band press the garment pieces, omitting the ribs. Tip: Take special care to press the edges, as this will make sewing up both easier and neater. If the ball band indicates that the fabric is not to be pressed, then covering the blocked out fabric with a damp white cotton cloth and leaving it to stand will have the desired effect. Darn in all ends neatly along the selvage edge or a colour join, as appropriate.

Stitching

When stitching the pieces together, remember to match areas of colour and texture very carefully where they meet. Use a seam stitch such as back stitch or mattress stitch for all main knitting seams and join all ribs and neckband with mattress stitch, unless otherwise stated.

Construction

Having completed the pattern instructions, join left shoulder and neckband seams as detailed above. Sew the top of the sleeve to the body of the garment using the method detailed in the pattern, referring to the appropriate guide:

Straight cast-off sleeves: Place centre of cast-off edge of sleeve to shoulder seam. Sew top of sleeve to body, using markers as guidelines where applicable.

Square set-in sleeves: Place centre of cast-off edge of sleeve to shoulder seam. Set sleeve head into armhole, the straight sides at top of sleeve to form a neat right-angle to cast-off sts at armhole on back and front.

Shallow set-in sleeves: Place centre of cast off edge of sleeve to shoulder seam. Match decreases at beg of armhole shaping to decreases at top of sleeve. Sew sleeve head into armhole, easing in shapings.

Set- in sleeves: Place centre of cast-off edge of sleeve to shoulder seam. Set in sleeve, easing sleeve head into armhole.

Join side and sleeve seams.
Slip stitch pocket edgings and linings into place.
Sew on buttons to correspond with buttonholes.
Ribbed welts and neckbands and any areas of garter stitch should not be pressed.

abbreviations & experience ratings

K	knit
P	purl
st(s)	stitch(es)
inc	increas(e)(ing)
dec	decreas(e)(ing)
st st	stocking stitch (1 row K, 1 row P)
g st	garter stitch (K every row)
beg	begin(ning)
foll	following
rem	remain(ing)
rev st st	reverse stocking stitch (1 row K , 1 row P)
rep	repeat
alt	alternate
cont	continue
patt	pattern
tog	together
mm	millimetres
cm	centimetres
in(s)	inch(es)
RS	right side
WS	wrong side
sl 1	slip one stitch
psso	pass slipped stitch over
p2sso	pass 2 slipped stitches over
tbl	through back of loop
M1	make one stitch by picking up horizontal loop before next stitch and knitting into back of it
M1P	make one stitch by picking up horizontal loop before next stitch and purling into back of it
yfwd	yarn forward
yrn	yarn round needle
meas	measures
0	no stitches, times or rows
-	no stitches, times or rows for that size
yon	yarn over needle
yfrn	yarn forward round needle
wyib	with yarn at back

Crochet Terms

UK crochet terms and abbreviations have been used throughout.
The list below gives the US equivalent where they vary.

Abbrev.	UK	US
dc	double crochet	single crochet
htr	half treble	half double crochet
tr	treble	double crochet
dtr	double treble	treble

Easy, straight forward knitting

Suitable for the average knitter

For the more experienced knitter

blanket stitch

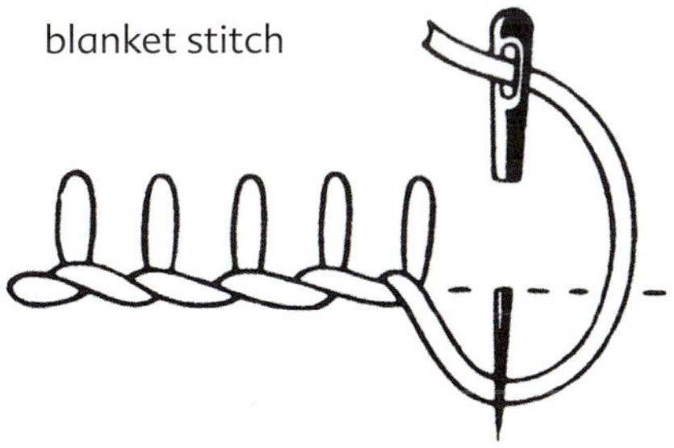

bullion stitch

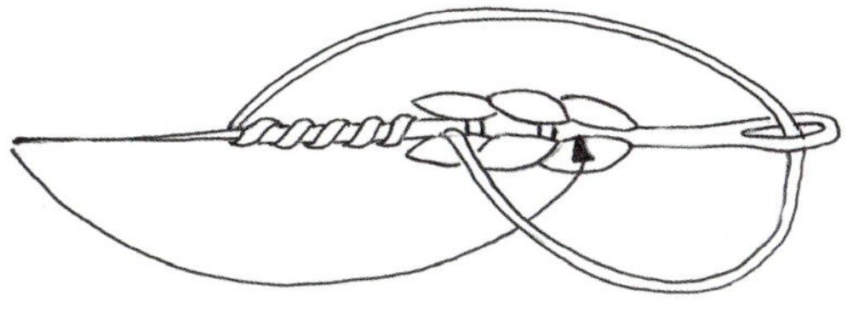

french stitch

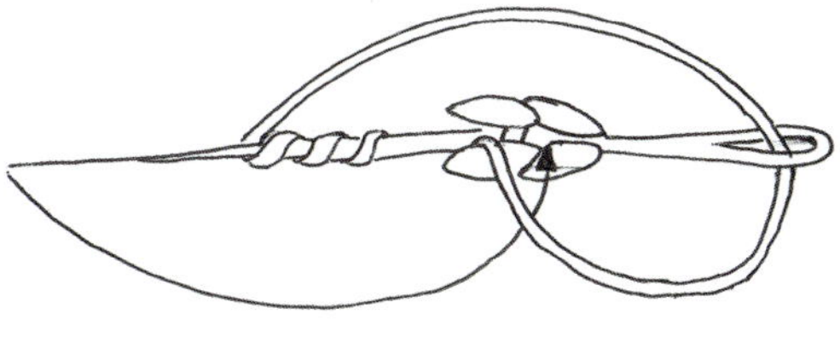

lazy daisy stitch

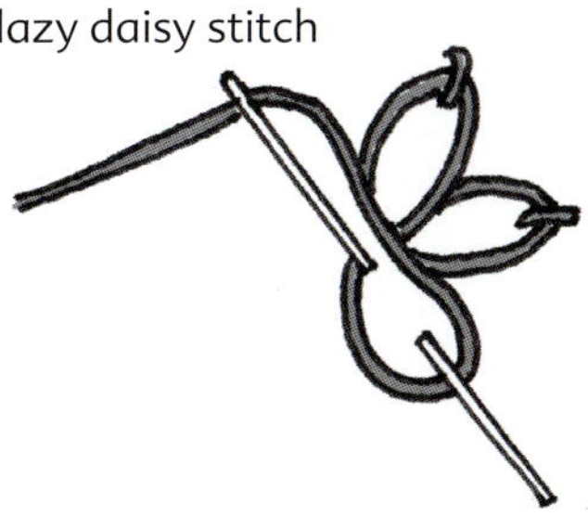

cross stitch a

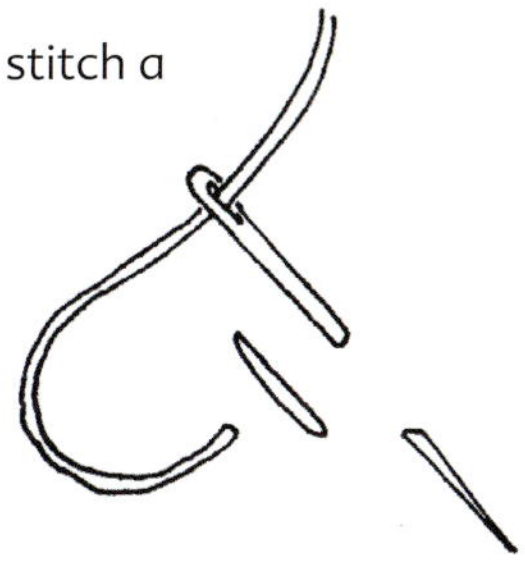

cross stitch b

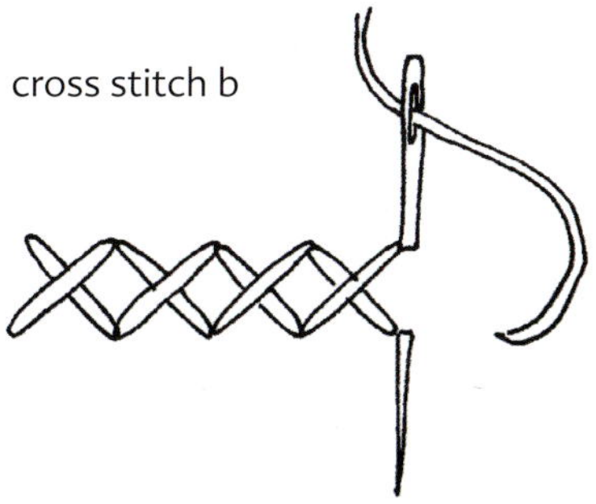

sizing guide

When you knit a Rowan baby or children's design, we want you to be happy with the look and feel of the finished garment. This all starts with the size and fit of the design you choose. To help you to achieve the correct fit for your baby or child, we have looked at the sizing of our baby and children's patterns. This has resulted in the introduction of the sizing chart below.

Dimensions in the chart below are body measurements, not garment dimensions, therefore please refer to the measuring guide to help you to determine which is the best size for your baby or child.

MEASURING GUIDE

For maximum comfort and to ensure the correct fit when choosing the size to knit, please follow the tips below when checking the size of your baby or child.

Measure your baby or child gently, close to the body over their underwear, but don't pull the tape measure too tight!

- **Height** — measure from the top of your baby's or child head to their feet when they are laying or standing straight.
- **Chest** — measure around the fullest part of the chest and across the shoulder blades.
- **Waist** — measure around the natural waistline just above the hip bone.
- **Hips** — measure around the fullest part of the bottom.

If you don't wish to measure your baby or child, note the size of their or your favourite jumper that you like the fit of. Our sizes are comparable to the clothing sizes from the major high street retailers, so if the favourite jumper is 6 months or 3 years, then our 6 months or 3 years size should measure approximately the same. Measure this favourite jumper and compare the measurements against the size diagram at the end of the pattern you wish to knit.

Finally, once you have decided which size is best for you to knit, please ensure that you achieve the correct tension for the design you are planning to knit.

Remember if your tension is too loose, your garment will be bigger than the pattern size and you may use more yarn. If your tension is too tight, your garment will be smaller than the pattern size and you may have yarn left over. Furthermore if your tension is incorrect, the handle of your fabric will be either too stiff or too floppy and will not fit properly. As you invest money and time in knitting one of our designs, it really does make sense to check your tension before starting your project.

STANDARD SIZING GUIDE FOR BABIES

AGE	0-3 m	3-6 m	6-9 m	9-12 m	12-18 m	2 yr	3yr	4yr	
To fit height	22 - 24.5	24.5 - 26.5	26.5 - 29	29 - 31.5	31.5 - 34	36	38.5	41	inches
	56 - 62	62 - 68	68 - 74	74 - 80	80 - 86	92	98	104	cm
Weight	10 - 14	14 - 18	18 - 21	21 - 24					lbs
	4.5 - 6	6 - 8	8 - 9.5	9.5 - 11					kgs
To fit chest					19.25 - 20	20.75	21.5	22.5	inches
					49 - 51	53	55	57	cm
To fit waist					19.5 - 20	20.5	21	21.25	inches
					50 - 51	52	53	54	cm
To fit hips					20.5 - 21.25	22	23	23.5	inches
					52 - 54	56	58	60	cm

AUSTRALIA: Australian Country Spinners, 314 Albert Street, Brunswick, Victoria 3056. ***Tel:*** (61) 3 9380 3888 ***Fax:*** (61) 3 9387 2674 ***Email:*** sales@auspinners.com.au

AUSTRIA: Coats Harlander GmbH, Autokaderstrasse 31, A -1210 Wien. ***Tel:*** (01) 27716 – 0 ***Fax:*** (01) 27716 - 228

BELGIUM: Coats Benelux, Ring Oost 14A, Ninove, 9400, Belgium ***Tel:*** 0346 35 37 00 ***Email:*** sales.coatsninove@coats.com

CANADA: Westminster Fibers Inc, 165 Ledge St, Nashua, NH03060 ***Tel:*** (1 603) 886 5041 / 5043 ***Fax:*** (1 603) 886 1056 ***Email:*** rowan@westminsterfibers.com

CHINA: Coats Shanghai Ltd, No 9 Building , Baosheng Road, Songjiang Industrial Zone, Shanghai. ***Tel:*** (86- 21) 5774 3733 ***Fax:*** (86-21) 5774 3768

DENMARK: Coats Danmark A/S, Nannasgade 28, 2200 Kobenhavn N ***Tel:*** (45) 35 86 90 50 ***Fax:*** (45) 35 82 15 10 ***Email:*** info@hpgruppen.dk ***Web:*** www.hpgruppen.dk

FINLAND: Coats Opti Oy, Ketjutie 3, 04220 Kerava ***Tel:*** (358) 9 274 871 ***Fax:*** (358) 9 2748 7330 ***Email:*** coatsopti.sales@coats.com

FRANCE: Coats France / Steiner Frères, SAS 100, avenue du Général de Gaulle, 18 500 Mehun-Sur-Yèvre ***Tel:*** (33) 02 48 23 12 30 ***Fax:*** (33) 02 48 23 12 40

GERMANY: Coats GMbH, Kaiserstrasse 1, D-79341 Kenzingen ***Tel:*** (49) 7644 8020 ***Fax:*** (49) 7644 802399 ***Web:*** www.coatsgmbh.de

HOLLAND: Coats Benelux, Ring Oost 14A, Ninove, 9400, Belgium ***Tel:*** 0346 35 37 00 ***Email:*** sales.coatsninove@coats.com

HONG KONG: Coats China Holdings Ltd, 19/F Millennium City 2, 378 Kwun Tong Road, Kwun Tong, Kowloon ***Tel:*** (852) 2798 6886 ***Fax:*** (852) 2305 0311

ICELAND: Storkurinn, Laugavegi 59, 101 Reykjavik ***Tel:*** (354) 551 8258 ***Email:*** storkurinn@simnet.is

ITALY: Coats Cucirini s.r.l., Via Sarca 223, 20126 Milano ***Tel:*** 800 992377 ***Fax:*** 0266111701 ***Email:*** servizio.clienti@coats.com

JAPAN: Puppy-Jardin Co Ltd, 3-8-11 Kudanminami Chiyodaku, Hiei Kudan Bldg. 5F, Tokyo ***Tel:*** (81) 3 3222-7076 ***Fax:*** (81) 3 3222- 7066 ***Email:*** info@rowan-jaeger.com

KOREA: Coats Korea Co Ltd, 5F Kuckdong B/D, 935-40 Bangbae- Dong, Seocho-Gu, Seoul ***Tel:*** (82) 2 521 6262. ***Fax:*** (82) 2 521 5181

LEBANON: y.knot, Saifi Village, Mkhalissiya Street 162, Beirut ***Tel:*** (961) 1 992211 ***Fax:*** (961) 1 315553 ***Email:*** y.knot@cyberia.net.lb

LUXEMBOURG: Coats Benelux, Ring Oost 14A, Ninove, 9400, Belgium ***Tel:*** 054 318989 ***Email:*** sales.coatsninove@coats.com

MEXICO: Estambres Crochet SA de CV, Aaron Saenz 1891-7, Monterrey, NL 64650 Mexico ***Tel:*** +52 (81) 8335-3870

NEW ZEALAND: ACS New Zealand, 1 March Place, Belfast, Christchurch ***Tel:*** 64-3-323-6665 ***Fax:*** 64-3-323-6660

NORWAY: Coats Knappehuset AS, Pb 100 Ulset, 5873 Bergen ***Tel:*** (47) 55 53 93 00 ***Fax:*** (47) 55 53 93 93

SINGAPORE: Golden Dragon Store, 101 Upper Cross Street #02-51, People's Park Centre, Singapore 058357 ***Tel:*** (65) 6 5358454 ***Fax:*** (65) 6 2216278 ***Email:*** gdscraft@hotmail.com

SOUTH AFRICA: Arthur Bales PTY, PO Box 44644, Linden 2104 ***Tel:*** (27) 11 888 2401 ***Fax:*** (27) 11 782 6137

SPAIN: Oyambre, Pau Claris 145, 80009 Barcelona. ***Tel:*** (34) 670 011957 ***Fax:*** (34) 93 4872672 ***Email:*** oyambre@oyambreonline.com

Coats Fabra, Santa Adria ***Tel:*** 932908400 ***Fax:*** 932908409 ***Email:*** atencion.clientes@coats.com

SWEDEN: Coats Expotex AB, Division Craft, Box 297, 401 24 Goteborg ***Tel:*** (46) 33 720 79 00 ***Fax:*** 46 31 47 16 50

SWITZERLAND: Coats Stroppel AG, Stroppelstr.16 CH -5300 Turgi (AG) ***Tel:*** (41) 562981220 ***Fax:*** (41) 56 298 12 50

TAIWAN: Cactus Quality Co Ltd, P.O.Box 30 485, Taipei, Taiwan, R.O.C., Office: 7FL-2, No 140, Roosevelt Road, Sec 2,Taipei, Taiwan, R.O.C. ***Tel:*** 886-2-23656527 ***Fax:*** 886-2-23656503 ***Email:*** cqcl@m17.hinet.net

THAILAND: Global Wide Trading, 10 Lad Prao Soi 88, Bangkok 10310 ***Tel:*** 00 662 933 9019 ***Fax:*** 00 662 933 9110 ***Email:*** theneedleworld@yahoo.com

U.S.A.: Westminster Fibers Inc, 165 Ledge St, Nashua, NH03060 ***Tel:*** (1 603) 886 5041 / 5043 ***Fax:*** (1 603) 886 1056 ***Email:*** rowan@westminsterfibers.com

U.K: Rowan, Green Lane Mill, Holmfirth, West Yorkshire, England HD9 2DX ***Tel:*** +44 (0) 1484 681881 ***Fax:*** +44 (0) 1484 687920 ***Email:*** mail@knitrowan.com ***Web:*** www.knitrowan.com

For stockists in all other countries please contact Rowan for details

notes

notes

• **Photographer:** Vanessa Davies
• **Stylist:** Marie Wallin assisted by Lisa Richardson
• **Hair & Make-up:** Lisa Richardson
• **Models:** Mary Greenhalgh, Andrew Klimcke, Neha White & Harrison Eade from Kids London
Georgina Miller & Michael Parker from Bruce and Brown
Many Thanks to Cory Hughes
• **Location:** Lavender Grove (www.beachstudios.co.uk)

With special thanks to the following handknitters:
Judith Chamberlain, Susan Grimes, Yvonne Rawlinson, Elsie Eland, Janet Oakey, Arna Ronan, Margaret Goddard, Helen Dawson, Barbara Wiltshire, Teresa Gogay, Maisie Laing, Carol Bayless, Joyce Limon, Jenny Cooper & Andrea McHugh

First published in Great Britain in 2008 by Rowan Yarns Ltd, Green Lane Mill, Holmfirth, West Yorkshire, England, HD9 2DX
Internet: www.knitrowan.com

British Library Cataloguing in Publication Data Rowan Yarns - The Milk Cotton Baby Collection
ISBN 978-1-906007-03-4